WILK

Stephen Brooke

Arachis Press 2020

It seemed a land of the imagination.

WILK
©2020 Stephen Brooke

ISBN 978-1-937745-71-4

Arachis Press
4803 Peanut Road
Graceville, FL 32440
http://arachispress.com

Interview, Part One

"I was born near Danzig," said the old man. His eyes remained turned toward the window, surveying the sea of clouds below us. "Gdansk, I should say, eh? It's Polish now. I'm Polish. But I grew up German."

His English was flawless. If he had any slightest of accent, it was indeed German. "Your family was Polish?" I asked. "Wilkins isn't the name you were born with." I had known this, to be sure, and my research had corroborated it.

He chuckled. "No, nor is Wilk. Patrokowski was our name. My father's name. Jan Patrokowski I was and officially still am, in Poland."

"Not elsewhere?"

"Not any longer. Things changed after the war." He turned to me at last. "The first war, the so-called Great War."

"You left Poland." I knew this too but felt it worth stating, for the record. Wilkins — or Patrokowski — could add more if he wished. I did not intend to push him.

A sigh. "I had no country. I was no longer German and I felt like a stranger in the land where I was born. All I had left was anger."

1.

How could he stay here? These Reds were intending to attack his own people, the newborn nation state of Poland. Not that Jan had any great love for that state or those people. He had even less for their de facto leader. He'd had nothing to do with Pilsudski and his plots during the war.

"I know you are not committed to the spread of our socialist revolution, Comrade Patrokowski," said his commander, a small bearded man in a voluminous and shabby greatcoat.

No, he had truly been committed to nothing more than fighting the British forces here, as he had elsewhere during the war. He had needed a target for his anger and they were handy. Now they were retreating and so was much of that anger. "I am not, Comrade," he admitted. "I think I should leave Russia."

The Russian officer considered this. "You know we can not permit you to join our, ah, adversaries." He might have thought to say enemies, and then thought better of it. "If that is what you intend, we shall have to intern you."

"I would go east. In the airplane I brought here perhaps." Such a plan had been coalescing in the back of his mind for some time. It was good to put it into words at last. So simple a plan, really, and one so difficult of carrying through.

"The Albatros? I'm not certain it is still flying, nor where exactly it is, for that matter."

Jan had somewhat reluctantly handed the old C-Three over to their fledgling air service when he had been accepted into the Red Army. Unofficially accepted, with no actual commission. He had flown a few reconnaissance missions early on, in a variety of craft, but mostly served as a courier.

And he had been a mechanic, and settled into being a teacher of mechanics and of flying, through long winter months and into this spring. It had not taken the Russians long to see where the young Pole's greatest talent lay and assign him to this flight school. "The Whites still control much of the way east. We would not wish you to go to them, either, but I will talk to my superiors," the officer promised. Jan nodded and turned back to the partially dismantled Salmson engine he had hoped to repair. That hope was fading.

Not until late the next afternoon was he called into headquarters, the commander's office. A fat young man stood beside the desk, clad in vaguely military fashion but with no insignia of rank. From the party, Jan decided.

The pair spoke briefly before turning their attention to him. Jan had picked up some Russian since coming here, but had trouble following their exchange. He had communicated with the Reds mostly in French. The newcomer addressed him now in that language. His accent was atrocious.

"Jan Patrokowski? Or should we say Hans?"

The official German papers he had carried on arrival had him as Oberleutnant Hans Patrokowski. "Either is acceptable, Comrade," he replied. "Or even Ivan."

"Have a seat, Patrokowski," spoke the commander, waving toward the two ladder-backed wooden chairs before his desk. As Jan sat in one, the party man took the other, turning it toward him.

"Do you know anything of China, Comrade?" the Russian asked. His tone was amiable, as one friend speaking to another.

"Very little," admitted Jan.

"We have friends there, and those we would wish to be our friends. Their infant republic has needs. Men who know of airplanes and engines are among them." A wry smile came to the plump beardless face. "And men without Russian names would find less resentment and suspicion."

"You wish me to travel to China?" That seemed to be what the Russian was saying. The idea was not so far from what Jan had been considering himself, though he had not carried it through to such a destination.

"If you wish. Not as a representative of our socialist republic, but unofficially. An adviser, if you will." He paused, to give Jan a conspiratorial look. The Pole half-expected him to wink. "We would also be sending an airplane or two with you. A gift will make you more palatable to the Kuomintang."

"So I would essentially be on my own there," said Jan.

"Exactly. A gesture of good will and nothing more."

And if he turned down this offer? Internment somewhere here in Russia, most likely. That could turn out badly. China was the decidedly more attractive choice. "Why not?"

"And thus both our problem and yours is solved. You needn't stay there, after all, if you dislike the place," spoke the Russian. "But that would be up to you. Our association ends at the border."

Jan nodded. It made sense enough. "Should I fly there?" he asked.

The commander laughed. "We can put you on a train at least as far as the front, Comrade."

Yes, of course. He had still been thinking of that embryonic plan of his own.

The representative of the party spoke again. "And how should we name you to our friends? Do you wish the name Patrokowski to follow you east?"

"We can give you new papers," the commander put in, leaning forward, elbows on his untidy desk.

It might be wise to keep his family name out of any official documents, Jan realized. "Make it Wilk," he said. "Jan Wilk."

"Wilk?" wondered the fat Bolshevik.

A chuckle came from the commander. "That is 'wolf' in Polish, isn't it?"

"A nickname I picked up in the war," said the man who was now Wilk. "I might as well put it to use — mmm, no, I think I shall use the French form. Make it Jean Wilk." He changed the initial 'V' sound of the surname to a 'W.'

Either way, it would be spelled the same on his documents.

2.

"I was a couple years into my engineering degree when the war started," explained Wilk. He and this Red Army man were managing to patch together enough Russian and German to understand each other. "Perhaps I shall finish someday." It might be nice to place Ing. before his name.

"You are going the wrong direction for that, Comrade," his companion allowed, taking another pull on the bottle of vodka before passing it over. The drafty boxcar shook and rattled, passing over an uneven section of track. Wilk hoped it would stay attached to the rails.

"Unless I go all the way around the earth. It might be interesting to see America." He made his sip from the bottle look more like a gulp, and handed it back.

"I hear bad things of America." The man took a swig and chortled. "Some I even believe!"

"Ah, yes, if the capitalists don't get you, the Indians will. I fear China will be worse, however."

The Russian nodded, his full beard wagging. "I am glad I do not go that far. Not that where I am going is so good."

This man, a non-commissioned officer, would be accompanying the aircraft they carried to the front. It was supposed that pilots awaited them there. Some of them might be men Wilk had helped train himself. Two machines were to accompany Wilk further, to the Chinese Republic. They were old machines, Russian-built Lebeds, suitable only for training. And then only if he could keep them operating.

Outside, on either side of the train, lay the awakening of a Russian summer. Wilk had seen a great deal of snow during his months with the Reds, through the Russian winter and on into the spring. It was good to see green again. It was drier beyond the Urals, was it not? Wilk knew as little of Siberia, he suspected, as his companion did of America.

He should get better with Russian, even if he was leaving the country. That was one reason he conversed when he would as soon sleep. And now he would have to learn another tongue. Mandarin. That was what the men in authority spoke.

But someone would speak German or French. He knew both better than his native tongue, and English almost as well. Polish was not used in the Patrokowski family home. He must write his parents when he reached China. If he had any sense, he'd be there with them now, back in school or helping to run the family's business.

Or fighting for a Poland that was at best an abstraction to him? Maybe it was better he was heading east; he could only pray that his parents were safe and well. As his mother and father, solid Lutherans both, undoubtedly prayed for him.

He rubbed at his beard. It would be a good idea to shave it before meeting any Chinese. He would look less Russian. Maybe keep the mustache. Keep the sidearm too. He was used to having a revolver on his belt now, though he had not decided how best to position it.

"I think we are nearing the front," said the Russian. "We should be by now."

Wilk smiled. "Except the front keeps moving eastward."

"Right. May it continue to do so!" He took another swig from his bottle and offered it to his companion. Wilk politely toasted to the Red Army's continued success. "Tukhachevsky is expected to retake Sarapul soon. Beyond there, who knows?"

At last report, the Whites still controlled the tracks beyond, across the Urals and on to their headquarters in Omsk. How Wilk would proceed once he reached the front was uncertain, had been uncertain from the start. A southern route had been mentioned, through Turkestan. Red control was more solid there.

He might get no further than those airplanes they accompanied, secured to a half-dozen flatcars. Avros, some of them, Five-Oh-Fours. Wilk had never flown one of those until he joined the Reds but had come to appreciate the machines. Would that he was taking a pair of them to China rather than the Lebeds!

China. It seemed a land of the imagination. It could as readily lie on the far side of faerie as it did across the wide Asian continent. Either way, it felt unreachable.

The monotonous hum of the tracks beneath them was putting him to sleep. Maybe the vodka could share in the blame, there, eh? Wilk closed his eyes only to be jolted into wakefulness the next moment. A sound all too familiar, the sound of war, had erupted outside.

His comrade cursed. Wilk's Russian was not good enough to know quite what the man said. He did recognize the "Angliyskiy" at the end of it. The machine gun mounted on a flatbed several cars ahead chattered. Where were the attackers?

The attacker. A single machine, dark against the clear spring sky. An Airco bomber? He knew the type but had never seen one in action. Not from ground level. It was banking for another run at them. Wilk knew about that sort of thing. It was what he had been doing himself a year prior.

His companion had taken up his rifle and stood squarely in the door, aiming it at the approaching aircraft. "Fool!" hissed Wilk. "Get behind cover!" The man took no notice of his words, but began firing, methodically chambering one round after another. This boxcar wouldn't be the target of the British attack. There were better choices, the engine, the airplanes, to strafe, to drop a bomb or two if they had them.

Indeed, the tracks themselves would be attractive. That might have been the objective from the start and finding the train but a bonus. The pilot turned his machine away from them, intent on making a strafing run down the length of the train. As he did so, the observer turned his Lewis gun on the boxcar. Wilk took cover at once; the Red soldier did not.

Wilk glimpsed the man pitching forward from the open door as he threw himself on the rough plank floor. More machine gun fire, fading, and then silence. No bomb? No airplane — it was gone. Perhaps the pilot dropped his bombs elsewhere and chanced on this train on the return from his mission. It would have been too good a target to ignore.

The train rolled on, persisting in its course. It was not going to stop. Wilk looked out the door, surveying the tracks behind them. No sign of his companion. Dead? Wounded? There was no way he could know. He found the bottle of vodka and returned to the open door.

"Here's to you, Comrade," he said, raising it before taking a long pull. "I'll say hello to America for you one of these days."

Interview, Part Two

"Did you see America?"

"Not then. Eventually. I worked my way home on ships, as a mechanic, but passed through the canal at Panama and on to Europe."

"After leaving China."

"Yes, after leaving China." There might have been a touch of wistfulness in John Wilkins's voice. "For the first time."

I knew he had been resident more than once. China was an important part of this man's story.

He looked out the window. "Still over the Atlantic?"

"We are," replied his wife. "It will be a couple hours yet to Paris."

"It's been a while since I've seen it," he remarked and turned back to me. "My first wife's father lived there for several years. Plenty of time to give you more, if you want it."

"The young man is coming with us all the way to Poland," Rita Wilkins reminded him. It felt good to be called a young man when one is pushing sixty.

"But I may not stay awake that long." Wilkins laughed and continued.

3.

"Those British pilots don't stray this far afield, as a rule. They operate further south."

"It might not have been carrying bombs at all," said the adjutant. "Maybe extra fuel instead."

Major Vassilevsky nodded. "Yes, on a reconnaissance mission, perhaps. It could be attached to the White forces ahead of us, you know, and not with the English at all."

The adjutant looked doubtful but made no comment. Vassilevsky went on. "The general has ordered us to take those Lebeds into our own service. He says we need them more than the Chinese."

Wilk could only shrug. "They're not likely to be of much use in combat."

"We're operating even more doubtful aircraft," the major assured him. "More coffee?"

"Thank you, sir, yes. It's been all tea the last few months." An aide refilled his cup from a pot being kept reasonably warm atop the wheezing radiator. Wilk stirred in a good quantity of condensed milk. He'd gotten in the habit of drinking it that way during the war.

"Ah, yes, we Russians are supposed to love our tea. So — what are we to do with you, Comrade Wilk? Your papers are rather sketchy."

"Intentionally so. They do correctly have me as a pilot in the German forces during the war."

"Fighters?" The major sounded hopeful.

"Of the two-seat variety. I wound up the war as second in command at a schlasta." The Pole's voice became almost imperceptibly firmer. "Understand that I will not fly in combat for your Red Army. However, if I can't be passed on to China at once, I am completely willing to work as a mechanic again."

Vassilevsky's nod revealed little more than acknowledgment of the statement. "Better than sending you to an internment camp," he remarked. "How about as a flight instructor? Some of the young pilots they send us are more than green."

Wilk considered the idea no more than a moment. "I could do this. I spent two months in the summer of Seventeen doing just that, after an injury."

"Shot?" asked the major.

"Bad landing." He could have added as a result of engine failure but saw no need for it. Let the Russians think what they wanted.

"Very well. Tukhachevsky approving, we'll put you to use. Never fear, Comrade, we'll be across the Urals shortly and able to send you along on your mission."

"But most likely without my airplanes." Not that they were a great loss.

The adjutant broke his silence. He had remained standing at his commander's elbow through the interview. "We could put Comrade Wilk on a train south right now."

Major Vassilevsky arched an eyebrow. "And route him through Turkestan? Definitely without planes then, and no trains cross into China there. No, we had best attempt to follow through on what the party had in mind for our guest." He leaned forward, hands clasped, forearms resting on the huge ornate desk. Wilk assumed it had been the property of some wealthy family, as had this country house now serving as an headquarters. The chandelier above them looked like it might have been used for target practice. "I'm glad to have someone competent here, no matter what his origin."

The adjutant's chuckle was tinged with nervousness. "Tukhachevsky says Poles are almost as bad as Jews. The fact that you served with the Germans is probably in your favor."

The major nodded. "Yes, our general likes Germans for some reason. As much as he likes anyone." He rose to his feet, extended a hand across the deep desktop. "We'll decide on your duties once you're settled in. Have someone see to his billeting," he said to the adjutant. Wilk shook the hand and followed the other man out of the room. A captain? He wasn't sure from the uniform.

WILK

It mattered not for he was at once handed over to an officer who seemed little more than a boy. Definitely years younger than Wilk's own twenty-four. The young man would be likely to see him as an old veteran.

And he was, wasn't he? "I am Nikolai Orkovsky," the boy announced. "Um, would you prefer we speak French?"

Orkovsky's French wasn't that bad. "If you wish. Russian will do. Unless you know German, maybe?" The young man shook his head. "Or English?"

"Oh, I went to school in England," Orkovsky answered in perfectly accented English. "You speak the language?"

"Adequately, I think. Better than my Russian!" And it wouldn't hurt to practice it. English was far more likely to be of use in China.

"You have been to England, Comrade Wilk?"

"No, my father thought it a useful language for business. We are a family of capitalists."

"I'll not hold that against you. My own ancestors were aristocrats. You might as well come to the house we pilots share." The Russian gave his worn satchel a glance. "This is all your kit?"

Wilk nodded and followed. The youngster was a pilot, then. He'd seen plenty enough like him over the past few years, coming fresh from school, and frequently dead within a month or two. War had a way of weeding out those who were not capable.

And those who were, too. Any man, no matter his skill, could be but a few seconds from death when he was aloft. He followed Orkovsky down the muddy road. A few soldiers huddled in the front of one house or another.

"We retook this village just a week ago. Our Red Army was pushed back last month but is regaining territory now." There was a note of pride in his voice when he added, "And pushing past what we held before."

"The army isn't here?"

"Well ahead of us. Here we are." The low-roofed house lay at the edge of the village. A farmhouse, perhaps, with what might be barns or stables around it. Beyond those, an airfield, uneven and muddy but in use. Aircraft familiar and unfamiliar, and of varied origin, sat scattered along its perimeter.

"The Air Fleet of the Fifth Army," announced his guide, waving an arm toward the field. "Part of it. Including the airplanes that arrived with you."

"Do you mind if I look them over?"

Orkovsky shrugged. "As good a waste of our time as any, Comrade."

The newly arrived machines were closest. A couple of them were a bit worse for their encounter with the Airco and its machine guns. "Some of these might be packed off again to the Ukraine. They're needed more down there."

"Once you defeat the Whites here, eh?" Wilk kept all inflection out of his voice, but assumed the young man would recognize it as a bit of jest.

"Exactly," replied the Russian in the same spirit.

"Hmm, a Breguet, isn't it? And I recognize the Sopwiths." There were a pair of the two-seaters. A truly ancient Farman sat beyond them. Wilk could glimpse fighters across the field but was not inclined to investigate them at the moment.

"Rumpler. Excellent machine. I flew them myself. Ah!" He walked all the way around the next aircraft in line, before nodding and breaking into a grin.

Orkovsky gave him a quizzical look. "You know something of this old Albatros?"

"It is the airplane I flew here from Germany last year."

4.

Wilk read the name on the ambulance. "Vow-shall?"

"Vok-sull." The man bent over the engine straightened up. "An English name and an English vehicle. I'm English m'self," he said, thrusting out a grimy hand. "Thomas Chapman, at y'r service. You c'n call me Chappy."

Wilk shook. The man had spoken in English. Word of who he was must have gotten around. "What's the problem?"

The answer came with a broad grin. "Damned if I know. I just drive the bloody thing!"

"I'll take a look, if you'd like." He peered into the Vauxhall's engine compartment, ran an exploratory finger here and there. "How do you happen to be here, Chappy?"

"Well, y' see, I was 'ere with the Expeditionary Force, up t' Murmansk, fightin' the Reds. And I says t' m'self one day, Chappy, why's we 'elpin' t' oppress the workers? And moreover, why are we in this bloody cold? So one day I just walked acrost the lines and joined up over 'ere." Chappy chuckled at the memory. "They didn't want t' give me a gun, of course, but I c'n drive."

"So you believe in the Bolshevik cause. Hmm, pollen," said Wilk. "All this springtime pollen is choking up your air intake."

"It's a blasted nuisance," agreed Chapman. "Makes me sneeze somethin' fierce! And yeah, I'm with the Marxist cause but, uh, maybe not with these Russians so much. Now that I've been around 'em a while, y' know?"

"I don't want to be with them for another winter either. I'm hoping to be on my way to China while the weather is still good. There, I think I opened it up a bit but you'll need to do a better job of cleaning it later. Take a soft brush to it, if you can."

"Sounds good. All of it, includin' China. Will y' give the ol' girl a crank?" Chappy got behind the wheel of the ambulance, fiddled with the controls. "Contact!"

Wilk gave the crank a solid turn. The engine coughed, died. "Again!" On the second attempt it sputtered into life. Running rough. If he had time, he might see about it himself. But airplane engines came first.

"'Op in. I'll run y' over t' the aerodrome. My main duty is t' 'ang around there and cart off the young fools what break their necks."

Or returned shot up. Better to do that than not return at all, though. "I'll have to see what my duty is going to be. Orkovsky is supposed to meet me." Apparently he had become the young man's responsibility.

"Orkovsky? I'd be careful with 'im." It seemed Chapman would leave it at that for a moment but he went on. "Not one of the fanatics, y' know? 'E's just an ambitious lad who knows 'ow t' talk the party line."

"And use it to his advantage?"

"Right-o, Comrade. 'Ere we are."

And there was Orkovsky. Wilk didn't bother to salute as he stepped out of the Vauxhall. He was not a part of this or any other army. "Am I to start in on mechanic duties? I know the German engines best, of course."

Orkovsky held up a palm in dismissal of the idea. "That can wait. We all wish to learn more about you first."

Just what did he mean by that? A number of pilots were gathered. He had met most of these men in their quarters the evening before. Two or three were veterans of the recently-ended war. The rest were youngsters getting their first taste of combat.

"Is it true you commanded a schlasta?" asked one.

Orkovsy turned to him. "You said you were second in command, didn't you?"

"I was, which means I did most of the paperwork." That brought chuckles all around. "But I flew my share of missions. That was in France."

"But you're a Pole," said another. "Why did you fly for the Germans?"

WILK

"I chose to fight for the Germans mostly because I mistrusted the intentions of the Russians. That I will admit." That he still did he need not mention. "And my upbringing was largely German."

Should he give his complete story to these pilots? It might be best to be honest from the start. "I did serve on the eastern front my first couple of years in the service. Only in the autumn of Seventeen was I transferred to the Schlachtstaffeln and went to serve in the west." At his own request. He could have remained an instructor.

"When the war here pretty much had come to an end," said one of the older pilots.

"And this one started," continued another.

"You flew a Rumpler, you said?" asked Orkovsky.

"Among other airplanes. I piloted one of the relatively few *Walfisch* in the east for some time." Wilk suspected some of the younger men did not know what that was. "Later an Albatros C-Five." With its unreliable engine, which he blamed for his crash and broken ribs.

They were slowly walking down the line of aircraft as they spoke. "A Nieuport fighter," he remarked. "I faced them a few times. A dangerous adversary."

"I've seen what I'm sure is a Nieuport two-seater with the Whites," volunteered one of the younger men. There was no reason to comment on that.

"And a Pfalz D-Three." Wilk stopped and gave the aircraft a looking over. It had the later, more powerful engine and other refinements, he could see.

"No one likes the Pfalz much," said someone.

"It has its virtues. About as strongly built as they come and able to pull out of dives where other airplanes shed their wings. Good for contact work too."

"Ground attack, as you were doing during the war?" Orkovsky asked. "You didn't use a Pfalz, I am sure!"

"No, a Halberstadt. I assume you have none of those." They would have been unlikely to show up here in the east. "I became acquainted with the Pfalz when I was an instructor." He looked the machine over one more time, before turning his eyes to the row of two-seaters facing them. There was probably little aerial combat going on here. It would be primarily reconnaissance and the occasional bombing mission.

"That is your commander coming, is it not?" Captain Mikhailov. He had met him last night, too, but exchanged only a few words. He strode across the field toward them.

"Comrade Wilk. Acquainting yourself with our aircraft?" His brief pause was not intended to give time for a reply. "I can assure you, as antiquated and shabby as they are, the Whites' are worse. The same sort of mix though. Orkovsky." He turned to the young man. "Escort Comrade Wilk to the workshop. Perhaps he can help keep us flying for another day or two."

With that Mikhailov turned and marched off again. "Well," said the lieutenant, "I guess I'd best introduce you to our mechanics now."

5.

"They don't quite trust you, do they?" spoke Chappy.

"So it seems. Mikhailov won't let me fly." Wilk gazed out across the mostly-vacant airfield. "Not that I've any reason to. And they took my sidearm." The Nagant revolver was heavy and slow to load but he had felt more secure having it on his belt. The Luger he had carried with him from Germany had similarly disappeared on his first arrival in Russia.

"I 'ave an unauthorized gun m'self. I c'n fix you up with one if y' want."

Wilk only nodded. Maybe later, if he felt the need. His attention returned to the empty field and the empty sky above it. Most of the airplanes were gone, off on a bombing mission. Chapman with his ambulance awaited their return, knowing he would be needed. Wilk would be needed too, to help repair any damage to the aircraft. The two other mechanics had at once recognized his expertise, especially with the German engines, and Mikhailov had given him free rein there, at least.

"Word is we pull out of 'ere in a few days and move east," Chappy continued. "The airplanes and the 'ospital. That's most of what is 'ere."

The village was also a staging area and depot, sending supplies on to the front. That was Vassilevsky's main concern. The major seemed to have quite forgotten about Wilk.

A man leaning on a single crutch approached along the roadway, picking his way through a maze of puddles. "'Ere comes Sharov," noted Chappy. He took a last drag on one of his treasured cigarettes before discarding the butt in the mud. "The man's not 'appy about still bein' grounded."

Fuming would have been more accurate. Sharov now called out, "Do I hear our planes returning?"

Chappy tilted his head, then nodded. "Back early, aren't they? I'd better get ready for 'em."

There. Not approaching from the proper direction for landing. "It's the Whites!" shouted Wilk. "Sound the siren!" This he directed toward the sheds, where mechanics and soldiers lounged, awaiting the return of the aviators.

Someone did crank the siren. By then, he was running for cover himself. The attackers might or might not spare the ambulance, regardless of whether they spied the large red crosses on it. They might mistake them for red stars. Wilk did not intend to linger and find out.

Nor did Chappy, who was close on his heels. He could only hope that Sharov was sufficiently mobile to follow. Into one of the two sandbagged machine gun pits he dove, before turning to see what was going on. That fool Sharov! He was headed for the two remaining fighter craft on the field. Both were ready for service; Wilk knew that. He'd looked after them himself.

"You know 'ow t' use that thing?" whispered the ambulance driver, nodding toward the machine gun. Why he was whispering, Wilk was unsure.

"In theory." It was a Lewis gun. Mechanically, yes, he understood it but he had never had the opportunity to actually fire one. Nor the Madsens carried by some of the airplanes. One of those was chattering now from the direction of the workshops with no apparent effect on the oncoming machines.

"I've used 'em before, but we're both noncombatants, eh? Best t' hunker down." Chappy did precisely that, curling up close to the sandbags. Wilk thought that might be advice to follow. He peered over the edge of the pit to see Sharov climbing into the old Morane monoplane.

He could at least give the man some cover. The Lewis gun was mounted on a rather makeshift pivot, obviously an infantry weapon with its air-cooling shroud, bipod mount, and shoulder-stock intact, designed to be employed against enemy troops, not airplanes. Wilk quickly rose, took hold of the pistol-grip, put the stock to his shoulder. Pull that back, right? Everything seemed proper. He let loose a burst toward the closest White aircraft.

21

WILK

From the corner of his eye he saw the Morane taxiing to a takeoff. Why did the Russian pilot choose the obviously inferior airplane over the Pfalz? Did he believe all the stories of it shortcomings or was he just more familiar with the monoplane? Fedor Sharov was no fighter pilot anyway. He had been flying two-seaters on reconnaissance missions.

Wilk cursed silently. He couldn't let that boy go up alone. "Take over!" he told Chappy and bolted from the emplacement. Whether the driver would, he had no idea. He sprinted toward the Pfalz.

Other than the German fighter, a handful of noncombat-worthy aircraft sat on the field, one of the Lebeds he had accompanied here among them. A Farman pusher, a couple of Avros still in need of repair. It would be no great loss if the attackers destroyed them — or destroyed the field for that matter. He shouldn't care. A bomb landed near them, its only damage a crater in the runway and a shower of dirt.

If the sheds were hit, it would be more serious. Would he have to start the engine unassisted? He climbed into the Pfalz's cockpit to set the controls. Ah, someone had run out to help him. "Contact!" he yelled out. The Mercedes engine came to life on the first spin of the propeller.

Let's be thankful for good mechanics, Wilk told himself, and turned his attention to the business at hand. An airplane was making a strafing run directly toward him as he lifted off. A burst of machine gun fire as he rose made it veer off. A Sopwith two-seater, obsolete in most parts of the world.

The attack was not well coordinated. That he could see. The enemy aircraft had seemed to pick targets at random and now appeared to be moving away from the field.

Of course. It would not have been their primary target. The White pilots might have been surprised to find it largely deserted. The supply depot — that was what they would be after and the attack on the airfield was intended to first deal with any defense.

Sharov was in trouble, a White fighter pilot on his tail. Some sort of

Nieuport, Wilk thought. Variants of the machine had passed through the flight school during the winter. He ascended toward the two. Most of the other aircraft had headed toward the village. Damn, this Pfalz climbed slowly!

Fortunately, the two fighters were moving closer to the ground as the Nieuport stayed on Sharov's tail, the Red pilot attempting to escape, turning, diving. Don't try to go too steep with that Morane, came Wilk's thought. Leave that to me.

Suddenly, the monoplane dipped violently to the left and plunged toward the ground. At the same moment, Wilk decided he was high enough and dove toward the White machine. He doubted the pilot knew he was there.

Steeply he dove, driving the Pfalz to dangerous speeds and releasing the fire of the twin Spandau guns as he closed on the Nieuport. He could see the smoke and the biplane spiraling toward the ground as he passed and pulled out of the dive, uncomfortably close to the muddy field. It would be of no more concern to him. Where were the rest of the White airplanes?

Off to the west of him, not that far, and close to the ground. Wilk headed their direction, keeping the Pfalz in a shallow climb. He should have some altitude on them by the time he got there. He could see the flash of rifles and machine guns below him but could not hear their report. It was to be hoped they would not mistake him for an attacker — with such a hodgepodge of craft flying for both sides, there would be no silhouette recognition on which to depend. Only the large red stars painted on this fighter.

Eight aircraft. All two-seaters? No, there was the unmistakable shape of a Sopwith Camel, close to the ground, making a strafing run. He had seen Camels do good work in ground attack in the closing months of the war. He also knew their pilots considered the Pfalz 'easy meat.'

It would be best to avoid it. Yet here he was plunging into battle. That was an Anatra closest to him, wasn't it? He dove toward it, released a burst of machine gun fire and banked away as he passed it, speeding on to the next enemy airplane. Shooting anyone down was less important than disrupting this raid, scattering the Whites and sending them running home. Wilk fired, turned away, sought another target. He mustn't forget those two-seaters, slow and outmoded though they might be, carried armed observers who could return his fire.

Plenty enough Lewis guns had been fired at him over the past few years. Best to keep moving. He loosed fire at another machine and then climbed away from them. The Pfalz might not have the best climb rate but it was better than any of those flown by the Whites. Except that Camel.

And it was coming after him. He wanted to get as much altitude as possible before the enemy pilot reached him. Enough that he could turn and dive at it? He looked down. No, not a chance of that. By the time he came around it would be on him. He made a wide turn to face his opponent, still with a slight altitude advantage. It came straight at him.

So he did the same. His shallow dive would be to his advantage and he should make a sharp turn to his right as they approached. The Sopwith's left. That was the thing to do. The compact Camel turned fast and tight to the right, thanks to its rotary engine's torque. Not so much to its left, and the nose tended to come up. All that could be taken advantage of.

Wilk banked off hard. To his surprise, the Camel did not attempt to follow but turned the other way, making a quick two-hundred seventy degree turn to the right, coming after him and gaining speed. The White pilot knew what he was doing.

He shouldn't engage with a veteran. And there was no point — the raid was at an end and the Whites were already winging toward the east. Should he try to dive away? He felt the Pfalz slip a bit as he turned again, one of its handling vices. It was also easy to put into a flat spin. Too easy.

As the Camel's guns raked his machine, he did just that. It was dangerous, Wilk knew, but it allowed him to drop suddenly below and away from the other airplane. That other airplane he ignored as his own now required full attention. He must come out of the spin before slamming into the too-close Russian countryside! The Pfalz was balky but he got the nose down, gave the engine power, turned the free-fall into a dive, pulling out too close to the ground for comfort. The other pilot had not pursued him. Probably off with the rest of the attackers.

Wilk returned the short distance to the airfield, remaining close to the ground. Two crashed planes burned in that field. Chapman was among those who ran out to him as he taxied the Pfalz to a halt.

"Sharov?" he asked.

Chappy only shook his head.

6.

"You have used up almost all the eight millimeter ammunition we had," said Captain Mikhailov, "but I'll not complain."

Wilk shrugged. "I don't know if it was worth it." He might have done better to remain grounded. And, he reminded himself again, this was not his fight.

"Perhaps not, in any tactical sense, but you certainly improved morale. Not only among my men but Vassilevsky's troops as well." Both paused for a moment to watch one of the planes taxi into a takeoff, then strolled on. "He'll be wanting to see you when we settle down in our new encampment."

"I didn't know the major remembered I existed." Wilk was not to be one of those who would shuttle an airplane there, closer to the eastward-moving front. He didn't mind. Riding with the other mechanics was fine with him. Or maybe Chappy would have room for him.

"I think I saw an old Aviatik among the attackers," he said. "I learned to fly on one. At the beginning of the war I might have claimed it was the most advanced airplane in the world."

"And I might have given that title to the Avro." The captain gestured toward a pair on the field, preparing to depart.

"Now that I've come to know it, I might even agree," replied Wilk. They had reached the familiar Albatros. "This machine's predecessors were pretty good too. You're going to fly it?"

"I am. I'll see you at the new airfield, Wilk." Mikhailov nodded toward the two man crew standing ready and climbed aboard. A minute later he was in the air.

Wilk could see no sign of Chapman nor his ambulance. That was just as well; he should help the mechanics and ground crew finish packing up and departing. A quartet of lorries, of mixed make and size, were being loaded. In an hour, he was riding in the back of one of those lorries, heading a bit north of east. Three other men rode with him and none seemed to know their exact destination.

"Somewhere near Sarapul, now we've retaken it," opined one.

"Nearer to the Urals everyday," remarked another. "Kolchak's army is on the run."

Wilk suspected they were more optimistic than warranted, but there was no doubt the Red Army was advancing. He could wait and follow the army east but would lose the summer. Wilk wanted to be off and away from this war.

Many kilometers, many hours, and at least three bottles of vodka later, they arrived at the new field. There was no village here, only tents.

"Wilk!" someone called as he slipped to the ground. Orkovsky it was. "Just the man. The commander wants to see you."

"Mikhailov?"

"No, Major Vassilevsky." The young officer turned and walked away. Wilk could only shrug and follow. There was still firm ground and grass here. That would surely disintegrate into mud in a few days.

The major's new headquarters were a considerable step down from his last ones. No manor house here; rather, Vassilevsky occupied one of the tents. Wilk did not see the interior as the man stood at its flap, conferring with his staff. He glanced up as the two pilots approached.

"Ah, Wilk. Tukhachevsky's heard about you. He wants to give you a medal."

"I'd rather he gave me a plane and let me continue to China," came Wilk's retort.

"I fear you are proving too valuable to let go. You've been noticed."

Wilk sighed. He had to agree. But he hadn't any choice, had he?

"Word will probably come down shortly as to the decoration. He may have me pin it on you. Um." The major paused. "Keep in mind, officially, you are my responsibility still and not attached to the air fleet. I could put you to work on my trucks until your future is decided, if you would prefer. Consider it, comrade." He turned back to his aides. Wilk was obviously dismissed.

Orkovsky gave a somewhat sketchy salute which was ignored. "Are you going to?" he whispered as they walked away. "Leave us, I mean, and keep Vassilevsky's lorries running?"

Wilk had been inclined to dismiss the idea when it was presented. Now he was not quite so sure. The dogfight had shaken him some. It had been unexpected. It had brought back memories he would as soon have forgotten. "I would need to think about it." Then he laughed. "I'll try to keep your airplanes flying for a few more days anyway."

Soldiers busied themselves erecting open sheds at the new airfield. Chappy leaned against his ambulance, watching, an unlit cigarette dangling from his lip. Wilk went to join him; Orkovsky hesitated a moment before deciding to head a different direction.

"That Orkovsky boy again, eh?" Not that Chappy — nor Wilk — had much age advantage over the 'boy.' "'E's not over popular with 'is mates. You've seen that I'd think."

"They know he has ties to the party." Wilk had recognized all that. Orkovsky was political. And ambitious. "But I don't think anyone actually dislikes Orkovsky."

"No, I suppose not. They just mistrust 'im."

Exactly, thought Wilk. He didn't trust him himself. He watched as Chappy lit his cigarette, slowly and deliberately breathing in the first of the smoke. The man was careful with his small supply and apparently never cheated on the number he allotted himself each day.

Maybe he did trust Thomas Chapman. "Word is y'r gettin' a bloomin' medal pinned on you," said the Englishman.

"Seems that way. I never expected to be a Hero of the Revolution." Both chuckled at that.

"I've got somethin' more useful t' you," spoke Chappy. He looked around. "It's in the back."

Wilk followed him into the ambulance. Litters were hung in orderly fashion on each side, and all was fastidiously clean. Chappy did not always live up to his public persona.

"'Ere it is." He pulled a long revolver from one of the chests. "I've one just like it. Smith and Wesson it is. The army used t' use 'em and there's still plenty of 'em floatin' about. The ammo too."

Wilk examined it. He had seen other Smith and Wesson revolvers, but not the model made for the Russian military. What, forty years ago or so? "Handier than a Nagant," he commented, handing it back. "Quicker to load."

Chapman nodded. "Better t' leave it with me for now. Wouldn't do for you t' go paradin' about with it on y'r belt." He slipped it back into the chest. "It's 'ere when y' need it."

"How much?"

"Only what it cost me. We c'n talk about that later." The man seemed to hesitate. "If you 'ead east, off t' China, I'd like t' come along. I don't belong 'ere any more'n you, Wilk."

It took but a moment's consideration. "Certainly, if the Reds are willing."

By the next morning, routine had set in. Planes came and went, Wilk worked with the other mechanics — but still shared quarters with the pilots. They now considered him one of their own whether he flew with them or not. But he was thinking about Vassilevsky's proposal.

Mid-morning brought two long automobiles to their field. That no one expected them was obvious. The lead vehicle was armored, with a machine gun mounted. The second was of the same make but appeared to be an unaltered touring car. It was open and one man sat in the back. Wilk recognized them as Daimlers. More British machines. Both passed by and pulled up before Vassilevsky's tent. The major hadn't expected them either.

"Tukhachevsky," someone said.

A crowd gathered as the news spread. The general conferred with Vassilevsky for a few moments. The major nodded, spoke to someone at his side. It was Orkovsky, wasn't it? He came straight to Wilk.

"You are wanted, Comrade," he said. "And it is too late to escape!"

Indeed it was. Wilk followed on his heels. Tukhachevsky was a striking sort, he noted as they approached, with a bold nose and prominent eyes — some might have said they bulged — beneath thick eyebrows. Orkovsky dropped back, took Wilk's arm to halt him, then took another step back as the general stepped forward, some shining bit of metal in his hand.

"Comrade Jean Wilk, for valor and service to the motherland, I award you the Order of the Red Banner." He pinned it on Wilk's breast and embraced him. "Despite you being a Pole," he whispered. It sounded like a jest. Wilk hoped it was.

Moving back, Tukhachevsky continued, his voice still holding the slightest note of levity — and perhaps of sarcasm. "The Party wants me to send you on your way, Comrade Wilk. I might even consider doing it." The general turned away from him. "Major! I have things to discuss with you."

Both disappeared into the tent.

Interview, Part Three

"The Order of the Red Banner?"

"There were some not-quite-official versions of it at the time. I am sure my name is absent from any list of recipients in the Soviet Union."

"He has had more prestigious ones pinned on him since," added his wife.

"And others before it," said John Wilkins. "I did receive my Iron Cross, after all." His accent was what some call 'Mid-Atlantic.' Not so his wife, Rita, a trim black woman with a head of gray hair. She sounded quite convincingly Australian, though I knew well she was born in Central America.

"My husband has been personally decorated by De Gaulle," she said.

He nodded in an amiable and possibly amused manner. "Yes. We got to reminisce about Tukhachevsky. They were prisoners of war together, you know. But that is quite another story."

7.

"Official word has come down," spoke Captain Mikhailov. "You are to leave our squadron and be sent on your way. And you will take two of our machines with you."

"I shall miss you," admitted Wilk, "but I can not say I am sorry to go."

"Understood, Comrade. You should go report to the major."

But Major Vassilevsky had no time for Wilk. His adjutant directed him to Nikolai Orkovsky. "He's been put in charge of you," was all the man had to say.

It was Orkovsky who found him, on his return to the airfield. "What I know for certain is that we are to fly down to Ufa and receive further orders there," the young pilot told him.

"Fly?"

"Yes, both of us. We're to take two of the Avros. I'll leave it to you to get them ready." Orkovsky's eyes strayed to the machines, at the far end of the field. "And as soon as you do, we can leave."

Wilk could scarcely believe that all this was suddenly going to happen. He had waited too long! "Tomorrow?"

"Yes. Oh, and Chapman's request to accompany you has been approved. He'll have to be your passenger."

Wilk had best go see the Englishman. They both must pack what was needed for a long and dangerous journey. Or so he assumed. There was no telling what orders might await in Ufa. He might again end up waiting for months.

It was now the end of June. If all went well he could be in China by autumn. But when did all ever go well?

He turned to the preparation of the airplanes. That was the most important task. Wilk was not overly fond of the rotary engines that powered them but felt he could keep them running. Perhaps an hour later, as he worked, Chappy came across the field to him, a duffel bag slung across his shoulder.

"I'm ready t' go," he announced. The man cast a thoroughly suspicious eye at the Avro. "And glad of it, though I'm not so 'appy 'bout the way we're travelin'."

Wilk remained perched on a short stepladder, looking down at the Englishman. "You don't like flying?"

"Can't say. Never tried it."

That was unsurprising. "Help me get this cowling back on, will you? I'm finished here."

Finished indeed. There was a farewell that evening, a few drinks with the pilots. Orkovsky was absent. "Saying goodbye to his mistress," one of the men told him.

"There's a different one to say goodbye to each time we move," added another. "Sometimes two."

Yet the Russian pilot was there at dawn, ready to embark on their journey south to Ufa. The flight from the camp should not be long. Wilk would have to depend on Orkovsky to lead the way, to choose where to set down on their arrival. Whether the man actually knew these things, he was uncertain.

Chappy was there too, smoking one last cigarette. "Calms me down, it does," he claimed. The man would have to be warned against smoking close to the airplane in the future, but Wilk saw no reason at the moment. "All our gear is stowed."

"Then climb in. And be sure to fasten your seat belt." In a couple minutes the two planes were aloft, climbing into a clear sky, the sun rising to their left. Their route was a little west of south. The countryside below seemed peaceful. No more than a couple months earlier there had been fierce fighting around Ufa. Now it was safely — reasonably safely — behind the Soviet lines.

There was a field, a pretty good looking field, with but two airplanes positioned along its perimeter. Couriers, more than likely, thought Wilk, as he watched Orkovsky descend. He followed him down, taxied to a halt near the other Avro, turned around to speak to his passenger.

"That's it?" asked Chapman.

"For now."

"For now is good enough." He unfastened his seat belt and hopped to the ground. Wilk followed. It was probably just as well to leave their luggage on the cockpit floor until they knew what was next.

"So here we are," stated Orkovsky, striding over to them. "I've no more idea than you what comes next, but we should report." The pair fell in beside him. "The order to send you off came down from Commissar Trotsky himself. He gave Tukhachevsky command of the Fifth Army so the general is inclined to listen to him."

"I'd like to know what the commissar has in mind next for us."

"We'll find out eventually. Ah, Wilk, what do you think of Tukhachevsky?"

"An opinion after one brief meeting?"

"First impressions. You surely have some."

"A man who likes to have his way. A dangerous man. Too dangerous to attach oneself to, I think." That was what the young man wanted to know, wasn't it? Whether he could make use of the general to advance his own career?

"So I think as well." There might have been some reluctance in the reply. "Here comes someone to welcome us."

Within ten minutes they were seated before a small shabby desk. One corner was splintered. The man behind the desk was not military. Or one might better say he was not a military officer; he was a representative of the Party, of the Bolshevik leadership. A surprisingly young man, perhaps no older than Wilk himself.

He was leafing through his own papers, after glancing at those Orkovsky presented. He nodded, put them down, began. "We are sending you to China with those two Avros in which you arrived, Comrade Wilk. It has been concluded they will make a better impression than the castoff Lebeds with which you started."

"I can agree with that, Comrade," he replied. It seemed the Russian considered him the man to speak to.

"We could send you by rail from here but you would have to travel west some distance before turning south and east again, and add several days, if not weeks, to your journey." A slight grimace. "That assumes the rails are intact. One may never be certain of such things."

Wilk nodded. He would not care for further delay. "So we fly? Or are we to be loaded onto lorries?"

"No trucks to spare, Comrade. It has been decided you should fly south to the Ural River and pick up the railway there. At, um —" He glanced at his papers. "Orenburg. You will be given the proper papers for this. And you, Comrade Orkovsky," he said, turning his attention at last to the Russian pilot, "are to accompany them at least that far."

If this bothered Orkovsky, he did not show it. Wilk, though, strongly suspected the man had thought he would be flying back north tomorrow.

"It is a long flight," Orkovsky said. "We may need to carry extra fuel."

"It's not likely to be the last time," noted Wilk.

8.

"My guess is they will put you two and the airplanes on a train east into Turkestan and me on a train west," said Orkovsky. The flight to Orenburg had been uneventful and had not even cut into the reserve of extra fuel they had carried.

"As long as it doesn't carry us anywhere there's fightin'," Chappy said, "I'll be glad t' board a train."

"There's fighting everywhere. But no British and no White Army where you are headed."

"I've heard things have heated up in the Crimea and Ukraine," Wilk put in. There had been plenty of news on the streets of this town. Plenty of rumor too.

"Which is far away," stated Orkovsky. "Far enough."

"And the White headquarters at Omsk will not be that far to the north of us."

The Russian laughed aloud. "Don't be such a pessimist, my friend! We'll have to trust Tukhachevsky to keep them busy up there."

Yes, they would. The news had also come of an uneasy truce in the conflict with Poland. Wilk could go home, maybe, if he wished, and forget about China. He was being pulled both directions.

"I want to put our layover here to use," he said. "I could add permanent auxiliary fuel tanks to our Avros. I don't know when I'll have another chance to work on the planes."

"Not till we get t' China, I 'ope!" said Chappy.

"The tracks don't run that far. We'll have to take to the air sometime."

"Or load 'em on a truck," muttered the Englishman.

There was time. Finding proper materials was another matter but Wilk felt he had done a decent job of it, working through the next morning while Orkovsky had been called to the military headquarters here. He returned decidedly dejected.

"I'm to go on east with you," he reported. "Tashkent, at least, or wherever we end up. I'm supposed to use my discretion."

"They've given you responsibility," Wilk told him. "See it as an opportunity."

"A very great opportunity to fail. My orders say to make sure you get to China with the airplanes."

His two comrades needed to think on that a moment or two. "Then you'll be comin' all the way with us, sir?" asked Chappy.

"Most likely. We're to get the Avros loaded onto the next train east. Or it's more south from here, isn't it? I need to see a map!"

"Not a problem," said Chappy, pulling a chart from his bag. He laid it out on one of the bunks in their quarters. "Southeast, it is, down t' this big lake."

Orkovsky looked, nodded. "The Aral. An English map, isn't it?"

"So it is." Chappy offered no explanation of that. "And then on east t' Tashkent. Hmm, Samarkand? We don't go that far, do we?"

"I wouldn't think so," felt Wilk.

"Not unless you wanted to end up in India rather than China," added Orkovsky.

"India doesn't sound too bad exceptin' I'd be shot as a deserter, more'n likely!" Chappy looked at the map again and murmured, almost longingly, "I've 'eard tales of Samarkand. A romantical sort of place."

"You probably won't think that if you ever see it," Wilk told him. But he thought he might well want to see the fabled city himself someday. "Let's get those planes to the railway. You'll need to requisition a truck and some men, Orkovsky." He gave the man a wink. "Remember, you're in charge of getting us to China now." And that fact had made Wilk's mind up. His two companions' fate depended on him heading east. Who could know whether he would have been permitted to return to Poland anyway?

Though the Russian officer had the authority to do so, it was Wilk himself who oversaw the men moving and loading the Avros. Before dark, both were secured to a flatbed railroad car. An hour later, they and the three men were traveling through the night on a long, mostly empty train.

On they traveled the next day, rising into hills that were the southern terminus of the Ural Mountains. It would be some eight-hundred kilometers to the Aral, and perhaps that much again on to Tashkent. Wilk studied the map Chappy had brought. "I think we should not go all the way into Tashkent," he told the others, pointing to a spot a little north of the city. "We can turn aside here at, um, Aris."

"Assuming a train is traveling east from there and the tracks are still intact," said Orkovsky. "But yes, whether we have to go into Tashkent first or not, we would want to get onto that track." The red line marking it skirted along the northern edge of a mountain range — a range they all knew from repute — before turning northward toward Lake Balkash.

"Too bad we can't go over those mountains," spoke Chappy. He sounded a little hopeful about the idea.

"Far too high for our Avros, I think. Maybe for any airplanes." Wilk let his finger trace the route. "This," he said, "is where we would have to abandon rail travel altogether." They looked at the expanse of rugged, desert country stretching between the lake and the border. And plenty more of the same lay beyond it. "And then on into China where it is to be hoped someone official will expect us."

The train moved slowly, stopped frequently, but it carried them. Until it did not. Shortly after seeing the northern shores of the Aral, they had come to a halt in a small town. The signs named it Kazalinsk. A river ran beside it and the railroad tracks turned eastward to follow that river's course.

"The tracks are out ahead," a young Red Army lieutenant told them. "It's the war with Bukhara. Several places are torn up." The boy sounded weary. "And no, I do not know how soon they will be repaired."

When he left them, Wilk said, "Get out your map, will you Chappy? I've been thinking about an alternate route and maybe we need to use it now."

The chart was unfolded. "You see, we could fly directly across the steppe from here to Lake Balkash."

Orkovsky perused the map, frowned. "About twelve-hundred kilometers, isn't it? Even with the extra fuel that's cutting things far too close. It might be better," he said, "to follow the river and tracks down toward Tashkent and attempt to refuel somewhere along the way."

"Perhaps," admitted Wilk. "Either is better than sitting here."

Orkovsky thought on that only a few seconds. He stood abruptly. "Agreed. I'll see about getting some soldiers to unload the airplanes immediately."

As soon as he left the car, Wilk remarked to Chappy, "We'll have wider expanses to cross than twelve-hundred kilometers later on. I suppose we can worry about those when we reach them."

"Maybe so, but I'm goin' t' start worryin' about 'em right now."

9.

Chappy returned with a long, cloth-wrapped bundle. "I figured it was time t' think about defendin' ourselves," he announced. "You and me c'n start wearin' our revolvers. And I found these for sale. Nothin' much but they could come in 'andy-like."

Two rather long rifles appeared as he unwound the coarse cloth. An old wool blanket, Wilk thought. That could be handy too where they were headed. He squinted at the pair of firearms. "I don't recognize them. Either one."

"This one's a Martini. Some of these were still being used in trainin' camp when I signed up for the army." He took the weapon up, levered its breech open. "Single shot but a good solid and accurate rifle. The pride of the British Empire not so long ago!" He chuckled a little self-consciously at that.

Wilk remembered the name from his reading. He knew little more of it than that. "I hope there was ammunition for sale too."

"Plenty of it. It's a popular gun in these parts and down in Afghanland."

"Good enough. The other is a Winchester?" He guessed that from its lever action. That was an oddity on a military rifle — which it obviously was.

"It is. I understand a bunch of these were made for the Russians early in the war. It uses the same ammo as their other service rifles."

"Excellent. We'll have to make Orkovsky reimburse you for them. And, ah, I think he should carry one of them. One rifle for each airplane."

Chappy reluctantly nodded an assent. It did make sense.

"Let's gather our gear up. It looks like everything is ready." Orkovsky had both planes out on the narrow dirt road paralleling the tracks. It looked barely adequate as a runway. If they loaded the Avros down much more, maybe not adequate at all.

"The tanks are all topped off," he reported, "and I filled some cans we can carry along too. I suspect you'll want to look the engines over, Wilk."

That didn't take much time. Wilk knew they were in good shape when they left Orenburg. His main concern was the air-frames — a bit of manhandling by an untrained crew of soldiers could dangerously damage a plane. But all seemed well. "Let's be on our way. You can carry this," he told Orkovsky, handing him the Winchester. The man had made no mention of the revolvers at his and Chappy's waists, though he had surely noted them.

Orkovsky looked the gun over and nodded in approval. "I know this rifle. I've used the civilian version for hunting. Do you think we need to turn the planes around for takeoff?"

"The wind doesn't seem much better the one way than the other," replied Wilk. "Chappy, you'll have to ground crew for us. I don't think any of these soldiers standing around would know what to do." And might hurt themselves trying.

A couple minutes later both Avros labored into the air and headed easterly, following the railroad tracks. Flat-sided cans of gasoline were lashed to the sides of each, in addition to the internal tanks Wilk had added. He was concerned about flying so low. It made them more vulnerable to ground fire, not that any was to be expected.

They passed over a crew working to repair a section of track. There were friendly waves. That was to be expected. There was no air war here.

Nor ground war, so far as he could see. But the destroyed tracks were evidence of conflict. The fighting was mostly further south, they had heard, where the Emir of Bukhara held sway. Wilk was allowing Orkovsky to again lead the way, choose where to land. They could probably make it all the way to Tashkent today if they chose to push themselves and their airplanes.

It was nearly three hours into their flight when the Russian dropped back and signaled that he intended to land. There was a small village below and what might be an army encampment. Wilk couldn't see

41

anything that looked like a decent landing field. It would have to be the road again. He followed Orkovsky down. It was dry country, the grass-covered hills rolling away toward the horizon, but willows grew along the river. The map had it as the Sir Darya or something of that sort. Maybe one of those words meant 'river.' He would ask about it later if he thought of it.

"We should be about halfway," was the first thing Orkovsky said on the ground. "Maybe we can procure more fuel here. If not, we can empty the cans we carry into our tanks."

"If we could replace all our petrol, this would be a good place to cut on across to Lake Balkash," Wilk told him. "We could bypass Tashkent and not need to loop to the south."

Orkovsky seemed to seriously consider it. "It's not essential we check in at Tashkent," he admitted, "but we really should. They might be able to send a message ahead to China. They should be able to provide us with more fuel or even put us back on a train. We don't know what might await us at Balkash."

It turned out the commander of the outpost was not willing to share any fuel anyway. Whether he actually had any, they could not discover. Orkovsky was ready to push on right then; it was not even noon.

"A couple hours rest, first," advised Wilk. "For our bodies and for our engines. I should probably look those over before we fly again." He know how troublesome the Gnome rotaries could be and wished he had all his tools with him. But the Avros were overloaded as it was!

Fortunately, the engines seemed little the worse for wear. Some, of course. That was unavoidable. It would be good to be able to check them over thoroughly in Tashkent, so maybe it was just as well they headed that way. It was still early afternoon when they ascended into the clear air. Four hours should get them to their destination. There was sufficient fuel for that.

The Avros handled better, being less heavily laden. They continued to follow the tracks; those seemed sound here. This morning, they had noted four places where they had been torn up. An hour or so along, they saw more men below them. Horsemen. Orkovsky could be seen waving toward them.

Suddenly Chappy leaned forward and shouted in Wilk's ear, "Those blighters are shootin' at us!"

So they were. He could see the flashes of their rifle muzzles as they passed over them. A whistle. That was a bullet passing close, maybe even through the fabric of the Avro. Did Orkovsky recognize they were in danger? Wilk revved his engine and pulled alongside. Chappy held up his rifle and pointed downward. It was assumed Orkovsky understood for he also increased speed and began to climb.

A sharp retort from close by. Wilk didn't need to look back to know Chappy had taken a shot with his antiquated rifle. Probably the only one he would get as they had pulled away from the group of horsemen.

Ha, Thomas Chapman had finally become a combatant! Wilk was almost tempted to circle back and give him another chance. He could not guess who might shoot at them but decided it might be best to fly a little higher from now on. From now until they reached China.

More towns appeared below and the country grew more rugged. The railroad tracks moved away from the river. A terminal came up and was passed over, with tracks leading both east and south. The town over there must be Aris. Soon the city of Tashkent rose before them, tinged red by the sun setting at their backs.

They circled, seeking a landing field. There, wide and welcoming. The Avros descended, the day's weary journey at an end.

Interview, Part Four

"My husband has always been fascinated with mechanisms." Rita Wilkins told me. "Especially engines, of course, but also guns. We compared our handguns very early on. I think it was his idea of courtship."

"Know your enemy," muttered her husband, with a wink.

"Had I been your enemy, John, you would not be here today!" she proclaimed.

"One of us wouldn't." Wilkins turned his attention back to me. "My wife is very right about my love for gadgets and machines and such."

"You mentioned you were studying engineering when the war broke out."

"I was, and I returned to it eventually. Mechanical engineering. I am entitled to place Dr.Ing. before my name."

"And he does," added Rita.

"Doctor of Engineering," I stated, again for the record.

"In essence. It's a European thing and not quite equivalent to an academic doctorate." This was stated flatly and without a hint of self-deprecation. "It has given me a bit of legitimacy in people's eyes, even when my actual business had nothing to do with engineering."

"Your company does research and consulting, your official biography states."

"It does indeed, and people have consulted me about all sorts of things."

10.

"Maybe rebels, maybe bandits. Often, there is no difference." Captain Kostov was a thick man, with a thick dark mustache. He had nothing to do with either bandits or rebels. Logistics was his domain.

"We can put you on a train to Lake Balkash, yes," the captain continued. "The tracks are intact the last I heard. They might be all the way to Omsk. You wouldn't want to go that far!"

"It would be a rather roundabout way of getting there," said Orkovsky.

"Indeed! But this flying into China — that seems unwise."

"We would have to have extra fuel," Wilk put in. "Ideally, a truck could accompany us with barrels of petrol." That, he knew, was highly unlikely to be. It didn't hurt to mention it.

"The problem with lending you a truck, Comrade," said Kostov, "is the uncertainty of having it returned." He leaned back, studying the high ceiling for a few seconds. It was a deep burgundy, set with tiny golden stars, except where the plaster was peeling off. "But camels are another matter."

"To carry fuel?" asked Orkovsky.

"Or to carry the airplanes themselves if you could dismantle them. Caravans convey many things through those deserts. They could carry you east across the mountains into Sinkiang, even, rather than going north."

Wilk wondered how many camels would be needed to carry two Avros, not to mention their engines. "What if we dismantled them and put them in a truck? That would cut down on the fuel requirement."

"Perhaps. I shall have to give this some consideration." The man rose and extended a hand. "Enjoy a day or two of rest while I look into what I can do," he said.

"Most amiable," remarked Orkovsky as he and Wilk strolled down the long hall toward the street. "And unlikely to do much for us, don't you think?"

"You can requisition things we need, can't you? Your papers say so."

Orkovsky sighed. "In some areas, there would be no problem. Here there is a well-entrenched bureaucracy to deal with. They can't be bullied or rushed."

They reached the open air. Tashkent was something new for both of them. Exotic yet squalid. "He might be right about a caravan, though," felt Wilk. "I'm not feeling quite so confident about flying across the border."

"But it would be quicker. Hmm." The Russian looked up and down the sun-drenched street. "I think I need to get to know this town better. And perhaps some of its women."

Orkovsky headed into what was the heart of the town. Wilk went the other direction, toward their quarters. They were fairly decent quarters, in what had surely been a private home at one time. Quicker by airplane? Not if they had to hold themselves to the pace of trucks — or camels — carrying fuel. There would hardly be any point at all to flying.

Only if they could be assured of finding fuel along their route. This he explained to Chapman when he reached their room. Not that he needed the Englishman's advice on the matter, but it helped his own thinking to put it into words.

Chappy listened, nodding from time to time, until Wilk finished. "I've asked around," he reported. "Trucks go t' China on a pretty regular basis. Camels too! I got a fellow t' show me on the map." It was already spread on the table, its curling corners held down with tumblers, for a breeze laden with the rich scents of Tashkent came through the open window. "You see, one of the main routes goes off the railway right 'ere." He jabbed a finger at the spot. "That's south of y'r lake. Don't need t' go that far."

"It's not far from there to the Chinese border. Into, hmm, Dzungaria? The name of the province, I suppose." There was a tremendous distance, he knew, from that border into the heart of China, though this chart did not extend that far. It was daunting. "I'm having doubts about flying."

"You c'n dismantle our planes, can't you?"

Our planes? That brought the briefest of smiles to Wilk. "Completely, if need be. Or partially. That would be preferable and enough if we could load them on a truck or two."

Orkovsky did not reappear till nearly dawn. Whether he had investigated the women of Tashkent, Wilk could not say, but he had definitely found its liquor. He slept almost to noon. No word had come from Captain Kostov nor anyone else in charge here.

But they were well taken care of and apparently considered important. Important enough they did not need to share quarters with military officers or government functionaries here, nor share their messes. Meals were brought to them.

"They're not sure what to do with us," Orkovsky explained over lunch. "I say, this coffee is pretty decent. Best I've had since, well, before the revolution. Anyway, I am told they would like to send us along as quickly as possible."

"So you were gathering intelligence last night," joked Wilk.

"Indeed I was. Most of the interest here is in dealing with rebels and rival factions. We're an annoyance."

"An annoyance?"

"But one that can not be ignored. The party leadership wants us across the border and after that we will no longer be the concern of anyone here." A long pause as he sipped his coffee. Orkovsky might have been thinking or simply savoring the taste. "Understand that no one in Tashkent cares about China, except that some of the Turkoman and Kazakh separatists have dealings with their counterparts across the border in Sinkiang. Which is not where we would be headed."

"Very well. Get out your map, won't you Chappy?" Wilk pushed aside the plates and bowls, and unfolded the chart before Orkovsky.

When he and Chappy had finished explaining the options they had discussed earlier, the Russian said only, "We had best find ourselves a truck. And a map of China."

11.

The truck Kostov had picked for them was quite inadequate. He had also demanded that one of his own drivers go along. Orkovsky had seemed to agree to all of this.

"Yeva has been able to find out some things for me," he told his companions. Yeva was a typist at the government offices. Orkovsky had spent the last two nights in her apartment. What her roommate thought of this, Wilk and Chappy did not know nor did they ask.

Wilk had not seen the woman. Chappy, however, reported her as being dumpy and wearing glasses. No matter. "There are better trucks available," Orkovsky went on. "And I could commandeer one and order it prepared for our use. My authority would not be challenged if I did."

There was something more here. "But?" asked Wilk.

"But I would be unlikely to get much cooperation on mounting an expedition if I run rough-shod and begin ordering officials around. Or worse, army officers! We need the good will of the local authorities."

"A few bribes c'n help with that," opined Chappy.

"Money in general can help with that. Even in a Marxist paradise. Fortunately, there is a modest sum on which I can draw. Yeva checked into this for me. I didn't know about it and it seems no one was going to inform me."

"So we can rent camels?" Wilk spoke it as a jest but knew it might be a valid option.

"If need be. But quietly requisitioning the truck we want and getting everything ready on our own would be more practical. If we present that as a *fait accompli*, I am sure Kostov or someone would be happy to send us along with it."

"Without having to do any work himself."

"Exactly. We might not bother to inform them at all and just take off! You're the one who knows mechanical things, Wilk. I'll have to depend on you to pick something out."

All three scouted for a proper vehicle the next morning, among a number sitting in an open courtyard. "This is the one Kostov chose for us," stated Orkovsky, pointing out a Ford. "Or one of his subordinates, more likely."

"Not nearly large enough. That one looks like your ambulance, Chappy."

"So it does. But built as a staff car." Most of the vehicles appeared too small for their needs.

Wilk stopped before one that was not too small. "Pu-card?"

"Packard," Chappy corrected him. "Accent's on the 'pack.' It's an American truck." He surveyed it a few seconds. "Or a car that's been converted to a truck." It had a flat bed, with a railing around it, and no cabin, the wooden bench seat open to the weather. Wilk assumed it was not the original seat.

"Just the thing to pack up, eh?" quipped Orkovsky. The pun was rightfully ignored. Wilk already had the bonnet open and was checking over the engine. One of the Russian mechanics wandered over.

Orkovsky headed him off, flashing his authorization papers. "We're checking over our lorry before taking custody of it." By that time Wilk had crawled under the Packard.

The man could see they were authentic orders. He hadn't the chance to see they named a different vehicle. "It's in good shape," he stated, with some apparent pride. "I just went over it myself." Wilk stuck his head out and nodded.

"Good enough then," said Orkovsky. "Do you have something for me to sign?"

The two went over to table beneath an awning. There was signing of documents from both men. "He signed my order without looking closely," Orkovsky confided on his return. "We might want to cross out 'Ford' and write in 'Packard' on it now, and hope no one notices."

"There's a simpler solution," said Chappy. "But let's get out of 'ere first."

Wilk nodded. "We will want to move quickly now that we've taken the truck. The Avros must be dismantled and loaded up at once." He looked over the Packard's wide bed. "We'll remove the wings. Hmm, undercarriages too, maybe, and of course the props. Let's head for the airfield."

A few minutes later, they pulled in beside the Avros. "I'll requisition some soldiers to help," promised Orkovsky, and strode off toward the nearby headquarters.

"And 'ere's my solution t' the problem of the purloined Packard," said Chappy, pulling out a folding knife and prying the automobile's metal logo off. "And now," he said, producing a Ford emblem, "we just attach this one I lifted. Most of these blokes won't know the difference." A bemused Wilk handed him a screwdriver.

It was not until after dark that the airplanes were stowed on the lorry. "Now we need to load provisions and gasoline," announced Orkovsky. "And then get this truck and ourselves onto a train north."

The provisions and gasoline had already been arranged. There had been little else to require their time these past three days.

"What of the driver Kostov wished on us?" asked Wilk.

"Chapman is an official driver, isn't he? I'll wager he's carrying papers saying so."

"That's true, sir," admitted Chappy.

"So we're all set and I'd best go say goodbye to Yeva. We'll start off in the morning! Oh, and I'll see to sending a telegram off to China to let them know where to expect us. The lines into Sinkiang seem to be working for the moment."

"Be sure to bring some money!" Wilk called after him.

"Yeva's seeing to that for me!" came the response, as the Russian disappeared into the shadows of dusk.

Wilk and Chappy headed back to their room and an early bedtime. I should have seen more of this city, Wilk told himself as he settled down for sleep. The window remained open. It was hot here in the days, the days of mid-summer, though it cooled down greatly in the nights. He could hear the city of Tashkent, still awake, still going about its own business, business that had nothing to do with a young Pole far from his home. Maybe he would come back here some day.

12.

Chappy had, in a small way, 'gone native.' He wore a turban and an embroidered vest he had traded for in the markets of Tashkent. "At least he stuck to men's clothes," drawled Orkovsky, on spying him so arrayed. Wilk thought the comment odd.

The Packard and its load had been driven onto a flatcar and lashed into place. They had decided it would be best to ride with it, at least as far as where the tracks split east and west, just before crossing the river and reaching Aris. It was important they all head the same direction there.

Yeva came to see Orkovsky off. Not at all dumpy, though short and well-curved. Maybe Chappy's description would become accurate a decade or two down the line. The roommate came too and gave nearly as affectionate a farewell to Orkovsky as his lover.

"You should have shared," was the only comment Wilk had as Orkovsky climbed onto the railway car. The train chugged slowly north. At last! They were truly heading to China now.

Or in a while, they realized when they reached the parting of the ways. Their train was shunted onto the eastern way and then sat while everything was inspected. Another train passed, headed west, off toward the Aral, and Russia beyond. An official came and looked over their 'Ford' and their papers before moving on to check the other cars.

"To be expected, I suppose," mused Orkovsky. "We are at war. Maybe they think we'll smuggle weapons in the Whites' back door."

"From what I've 'eard, most of the folks on this train are traders, 'eadin' the same way we are," said Chappy. "'Ey, it sounds like we're ready t' get movin'." A whistle sounded ahead of them, the train lurched, stopped, then began to slowly move forward. "Next stop, some place I can't pronounce!"

There were several stops, some at villages, some in desert wilderness, but there was loading to be done at most of them and no one seemed to hurry. Orkovsky took advantage of the halts to go sit in other cars, mostly boxcars or flatbeds, as their own, and converse with their fellow travelers. These were predominately Turkoman and Kazakh. Most knew Russian.

"Many will be getting off where we do," he reported back. "The beginning of the great caravan route into China. Or the end of the great caravan route into Turkestan. We're coming up to a stop at Alma Ata now, before the tracks cross the Ili River."

Two rivers they had already crossed, flowing through a near-desert landscape of scrub-covered hills. Chappy got out his map. Both maps; they had one for China now but the names were all in Russian and Cyrillic letters, which neither he nor Wilk read. "We follow this Ili, it looks like," he reported.

The report of a gun startled them. Two or three shots, then silence. "Some disgruntled tribesman taking a potshot at the train, most likely," said Orkovsky. "I was warned to expect that sort of thing." A slightly wry smile. "There will be much more danger when we start traveling east."

They had all known that. There was no point in mentioning it, thought Wilk. They had their guns, they would be traveling with a caravan. Nothing more was to be done. Still, he wished he were able to fly and be across the border swiftly, leaving these arid plains and mountains behind.

There was a layover of nearly an hour at Alma Ata. It was a larger village, maybe even a town. There were troops there. Their papers were checked again.

"Another two-hundred kilometers," a fellow traveler informed them. "We must cross the high bridge."

"We will stop even longer then," added his companion. Wilk assumed the pair were Turkomans. They dressed like Turkomans but spoke better Russian than he. "All the trucks will have to be unloaded."

"And others loaded on. That is as far as this train goes, for now. The Whites hold the lands further north. Supposedly."

"I doubt the tracks are still intact." Both men nodded at that.

WILK

"We used to trade up that way," the first man went on. "I am Kazimir." He nodded toward his companion. "My brother-in-law."

"Call me Adrik."

"And call me Kolya," spoke Nikolai Orkovsky, extending a hand. "These foreigners are Wilk and Chappy."

"We are all foreigners when we cross into China," remarked Adrik. He was squat and dark, and had a thin beard that did not at all hide his smile. Kazimir was short too, but slender, and his eyes were gray.

The train whistle blew a warning. "Time to board again." They went their ways, Wilk and his companions back to their truck, the other two into one of the boxcars.

"The word is those two are opium smugglers," Orkovsky reported. "They buy in Tashkent and bring it north and then into China."

"And it is common knowledge?" asked Wilk. He found it hard to believe; even now, despite what he had seen over the past few years, things alien to him popped up.

"They undoubtedly pay quite a few bribes." Chappy nodded knowingly at this.

The train slowly picked up speed.

13.

Cars were uncoupled, one by one as the train slowly moved forward, so vehicles could be rolled off, on boards that looked far too flimsy and narrow to Wilk. Chappy handled the debarking of their Packard with aplomb. Animals were led from other cars, horses and camels. Boxes and bales were handed down. There was a process and it was not hurried.

And then they were reloaded with new cargo, fresh from caravans returning from the east. Fewer animals.

Wilk surveyed the herds. "It is a good time to take these east," spoke Kazimir, coming up beside him. "The cold weather is not so far away in this part of the world. I have camels to carry my goods but will try to sell most before returning."

"We have heard rumors of your goods."

Kazimir shrugged. "Such rumors are to be neither denied nor admitted. We carry medicines too, medicines hard to come by in the western provinces of China. Maybe in the rest of China, too. I wouldn't know as I never go that far. That makes it others' business. Also, precious stones. Semi-precious. Crystals. Sometimes lapis. A few carpets. Whatever seems likely to turn a profit. There are many such as we on this road."

"I read romances as a boy of caravans traversing the desert. Here I am in the exotic East of those tales." He gazed at the bustle all about them. "They did not mention the stench of the camels."

"The winds will carry that away when we are traveling. Some! You and your friends will remain with us? It is not good to go on by ones self, though some who drive trucks choose to hurry ahead."

"It would seem wise to stay with the caravan." He would certainly advise Orkovsky so, even if it slowed them. No, he would tell him so. "But the road is much traveled, is it not?"

"It is. Not so much as the fabled Silk Road. That way runs further south, from Tashkent across the mountains into Sinkiang. We will meet it in time."

Wilk nodded. He had studied the maps over and over these past weeks. "Our first thought was to follow that route but we were certain our airplanes were not capable of such a flight. Perhaps this truck could have made it."

"Possibly. Trucks do cross but I would trust a camel more. Ah, here comes my best camel-driver. Is all ready?"

A slender boy approached. "It is, Father. Uncle Adrik is set to go home."

Kazimir turned to Wilk, telling him, "Adrik returns to Tashkent to tend our affairs there. Wilk, allow me to introduce you to my daughter, Axana."

"Wilk? What sort of name is that?" the girl demanded. There could be a girl under the loosely-fitting colorless male garments.

"Polish. It means Wolf. But I go by Jean."

"Jean? That's Ivan in Russian, isn't it? I never liked that name. I'll call you Loup." Apparently Axana knew some French.

Kazimir sighed. "She probably will. By the way, I am better known as Kasim on these roads."

The train was beginning to back up, coupling the cars again. Wilk thought he had seen a siding back at Alma Ata where the engine could be turned to Tashkent. That was no concern of his now.

"I'd better go see if my own traveling companions are prepared," he announced. "By the way, you'd do well to keep your Axana hidden from Kolya. Or tell him she's a boy."

"Ah, but then I would have to worry about your Chappy, wouldn't I?" The man laughed and strolled off beside his daughter.

Chappy? Wilk recalled Orkovsky's earlier offhand remark. Was there a side to the Englishman of which he hadn't been aware? Perhaps that was no concern of his either.

It was not such bad country here. Wilk had noted occasional green fields along their way as they came north. Some, in fact, lay close by now, though more had been back closer to the Ili River. Irrigated, no doubt.

He had mentioned it to his comrades. "From a distance I would guess it is millet," Orkovsky told him. Wilk had no idea what millet looked like so he took the Russian's word. There were sheep too. Wilk had spied a great many sheep so far on his journey from Russia.

Now those comrades were ready to go. He did not regret having left them the task of preparation; as Orkovsky earlier, he had been learning things. That was important.

But he was definitely going to look everything over before they started east. First the provisions. That was most important. Then the airplanes.

Of course, all that had been checked over before they embarked from Tashkent, and one or another of them had kept an eye on the Packard since. Still — best to be safe. Chappy sat behind the wheel, waiting. "I 'ope we know what we're doin'," he commented.

"We still may need to take to the air at some point," replied Wilk, checking the cans of petrol. If anyone had a mind for theft, they would be the most obvious target. "If we do, this was the better choice."

Nothing seemed missing, everything seemed in place. The Avros? The sound of hooves made him look up.

"Come along, Loup!" called Axana. She was seated on a shaggy pony. Her eyes, light like her father's, swept across the other two, with seeming disinterest. "You need to fall in behind us. Then you can smell camels all the way to China!" With one bark of a laugh, she wheeled her mount and cantered off.

"Follow that girl," ordered Wilk. He could check over the airplanes anytime. Even in China.

Orkovsky turned around to peer at him. "Who was that?"

"That is Kasim's daughter. Kazimir's daughter. Do not get us into trouble with her or he is likely to lead us into the Gobi and abandon us there. Now get out and crank the engine."

Interview, Part Five

"Loup. That is what you chose to name your business."

"Yes, Loup Limited, when I settled for good in Australia. That was after the Second War. My children run it now." He gave me a bit of a wink. "As you well know."

Rita had to add, "And grandchildren."

"But I used the name here and there over the years. Not for myself." That brought a fleeting smile. "At least not often. Jean Loup sounds rather ridiculous."

I chose not to comment on that, though I was inclined to agree. "Loup Limited. Would you tell me of it?"

"Research and consulting, as advertised." John Wilkins chuckled. "And a bit of spying, at one time. Or so some might call it. That is not really in our line anymore. I first set the company up right after the war to consult with those interested in doing business in the Far East. That was always our primary stock in trade."

"In Forty-six."

"I suppose so. Does that sound right to you?" he asked his wife.

"That's what the documents hanging on our office walls say," replied Rita. "You were established in your trade by the time I met you in Forty-eight."

"Yes. A good year." Wilk gave her a wink. Then, abruptly, "I did use the name 'Loup' when I served as a fighter pilot with the Chinese, to provide some distance from my family there. We were flying Gladiators. Outclassed." He shook his head. "That was in the late Thirties. But it does all go back to Axana. I named my plane after her. A warrior in the wind."

14.

"When the Reds are victorious your way of doing business will be at an end. Your way of living will be at an end."

"Maybe so, Kolya, maybe so. *If* you Reds are victorious."

"They will be," said Wilk. "That seems certain now. How quickly they can change things is less certain."

Kasim gave an emphatic nod to this. "It is difficult to sweep away old customs overnight."

Orkovsky only smiled. "You may feel different when they collectivize your camel herd."

"Not while bullets remain in my rifle!" proclaimed Axana. She sounded quite vehement. Her father could not help laughing.

"All fourteen of them?" he asked. "I hope to have fewer than half that number on my return."

"What do you bring back?" asked Chappy. This conversation was, seemingly of necessity, in Russian. "If you mind, um, mind not the asking."

"I do not. You are not my competition! Porcelains, sometimes. Much of the traditional trade from China — tea, silks, that sort of thing — no longer offers much profit. It will be worse when the railroads to the north are open again. That may truly mean an end to our way of life, Kolya, whoever is in power." He rose. "I am going to relieve Jagatai." That was the other camel-driver, a young hired man, and a Mongol, not a Turkoman. Kasim had picked him up on some previous trip east.

As soon as he was gone, Axana told them, "Father speaks English perfectly well, so watch your talk around him."

"And do you?" asked Wilk.

She smiled. "I have picked up some from him. He learned it dealing in the south. One must know English there."

"But you know French."

Axana giggled, seemingly embarrassed. "Less than English. I have tried to read French novels with the aid of a dictionary. I've almost made it all the way through *Mauprat*! But I've never had anyone to speak it with." She brightened. "I *am* fluent in Mandarin."

They fell into silence. There was no fire, only a small kerosene lantern. The sky was incredibly dark, thought Wilk, the stars showing brighter against its blackness than ever he could remember them. The temperatures were dropping rapidly too.

All the day they had climbed toward the mountains and the border. That lay some two-hundred kilometers from where the road left the railway. A distance they might readily have covered in a day in their truck — camels took longer.

Other dim lights were scattered about their campground. Two dozen or more traders were in this group of companions, most traveling on horse or camel. Some other motor vehicles had gone ahead more quickly. Wilk felt he had done well to keep to this more leisurely pace, remaining among those familiar with the road.

Horse traders traveled with them, and camel traders too, both with their herds. A variety of goods were being transported. Saffron from far away. Dates from closer. Leather goods. Sewing machines. Precious gems. Even coffee.

And all had guns. Those too could be traded, they were told, if one did not become greedy and try to carry too many across the border. Officials expected one to have an extra rifle or two. There were dangers on the road.

Jagatai joined them, wordlessly. He had only a little Russian, anyway, and some Chinese, mostly conversing with Kasim in a broken Turkic pidgin. The Mongol was very young, perhaps even younger than Axana, whom Wilk guessed at being yet in her teens.

Did the girl have a husband somewhere? It would be unusual for a woman of her age to remain unmarried in this part of the world. But her father was no traditionalist. Nor was Axana, with her Russian name and her French novels.

It was not anything Wilk need concern himself with. "Should we help watch the animals?" he asked.

"You would just get in the way," Axana informed him. "Leave that to those who herd them." Wilk had noted that everyone's camels and horses were kept together through the night. It surely made it easier to keep watch on them.

She continued. "They are most common target for thieves, who attempt to slip away with one or two in the dark. But do not think they won't steal everything in your truck, given the opportunity." Axana yawned. "I am for my blankets." Without further words, she rose and left them.

"We all should be," said Orkovsky.

The night was cool. It would be cooler tomorrow night, when they were higher up. Chappy chose to sleep beneath the Packard. It stood well off the ground and provided some shelter. Not that shelter was needed on this clear star-filled night. Wilk wrapped himself in his blankets and settled down nearby. The milling of the beasts of burden was a subdued murmur in the dark, a word or laugh rising above it now and again as all the camp fell into sleep. All save the few sentries keeping watch.

Should one of them remain awake too? They could make up for lost sleep in the truck tomorrow, after all. This thought faded from Wilk's mind and into the night.

His eyes opened. Was it dawn? No, the camp still slept about him, as the rounded hills lay sleeping about the camp. But something moved before them, the shape of a man, stealthily mounting the rear of the truck.

"Hold there!" Wilk cried out. The shadow did not hold but immediately leaped down and ran into the darkness. Chappy rolled from beneath the truck bed, a revolver in his hand. It was prudent to sleep with it. Wilk would remember to keep his close from now on.

"What was it?" asked the Englishman.

"A thief. After the petrol, I would think." Anyone would have known a truck carried extra fuel on this road. "It's a good thing I'm a fitful sleeper but one of us should stay on guard from now on."

WILK

One of the men camped near them, roused by the noise — not that there had been much — came over and spoke in Russian. "Travelers new to the road may not be cautious enough. There are those who recognize this and try to take advantage of it." The Turkoman yawned, stretched, looked to the sky. "An hour and more yet." With that he returned to his blankets.

Orkovsky had apparently heard nothing and slept on, his blankets pulled over his head. Wilk and Chappie knew they would not fall asleep again. They sat and waited wordlessly for their traveling companions to arise. That began before there was any sign of the sun's rising.

Around the camp, men stirred, preparing for their departure, making tea on kerosene stoves or small charcoal burners. There was no wood for fires along this road. "We can fry ourselves bacon soon," quipped Orkovsky, heating water for coffee on their own stove. "We'll be out of Muslim country and into Buddhist."

"Ah," spoke Kasim who had silently joined them, "but you will still travel with followers of the Prophet." He took a cross-legged seat beside Wilk. "You rise in the esteem of those fellow travelers. Word of your encounter last night has already spread through the camp."

"They appreciate those what c'n take care of themselves, eh?" asked Chappy. "Just 'o do y' reckon was after our stuff?"

"Most likely, one who lurks in this place, looking to prey on passers-by. But it could have been one who travels with us." Kasim gave them a crooked grin. "Those are more likely to wait for better chances later on."

He rose. "We press on to Dzharkent today, if possible. It may be necessary to remain there a short time, while the officials inspect everything. It is the last Russian outpost before we go through the gap to China."

15.

The Russian officials needed only glance at the papers Orkovsky presented. They were not going to stand in the way of Party business. It was another matter for Kasim and many of the others. There were new bureaucrats in charge, men appointed by the Reds.

New bribes would have to be worked out, or ways of circumventing those who insisted on remaining honest. Kasim's medicine was particularly a point of contention. Its documentation was not at all adequate, felt the inspector. In his concern over it, he did not seem to note the other 'medicine' Kasim was reputed to carry. In the end, a fairly hefty fee need by paid.

Kasim swore greatly. Also he admitted later it could have been worse. "At least we are likely to see familiar faces across the border." That brought another thought to the trader's mind. "I should lend you Axana as translator when we reach China. Some officials speak Russian but some do not. The Chinese are often contemptuous of those who can not speak Mandarin. We are all barbarians to them!"

"Better yet," said Wilk, "I might ask her to teach me that language. I am going to need it."

Kasim gave this a brief consideration. "Can you ride, Wilk? Axana is on horseback most of the day."

"After a fashion. I would seem a clumsy rider to you, I am sure." And to Axana and Jagatai and most of the others with whom they traveled.

"As I seem clumsy to many of those we will meet across the mountains. The Mongols are born on horseback, or so they claim. It must pain their mothers greatly! I am willing to lend you a horse from time to time. What price Axana might ask for lessons, however, I can not say."

"Orkovsky, um, has funds at his disposal. Perhaps we should buy a horse or two."

"Ah, Kolya carries gold, maybe? Best to let none know that." Kasim laughed. "Me included! I tell you, my friend, I thought maybe to steal your truck and airplanes and leave you in the desert, but my daughter likes you." Wilk was fairly certain Kasim meant it as a joke.

It was later than most of the traders would have wished — and much grumbling rose about it — but they were on the road again by mid-morning, following a night camped at Dzharkent. The road was in good condition and rose steeply through the day, into a high gap between the peaks. The Packard came perilously close to overheating.

"It's the thin air, it is," felt Chappy. "The old girl should make it if we don't push 'er too 'ard." The Avros were not that heavy — the engines and the extra fuel added the most weight. The fuselages extended some distance beyond the bed of the truck and the wings further yet, requiring some caution on the uneven roadway. Their progress was slow enough that Orkovsky and Wilk walked alongside the truck. Many of the horses were being led, too, at least from time to time.

"The map shows this as one of the highest points of our journey," Orkovsky informed them. "And it doesn't compare with crossing the Terek Pass into Sinkiang." He was looking over their map, the one of China, as they marched along. The wind whistling up the narrow way between the mountains threatened to tear it from his hands. "All down-hill in China. Hmm, well a little of going up here and there, and especially when we get in as far as —" He strained to make out a name. "Hami." He looked up. "I may not be with you by then. Strictly speaking I only am ordered to get you across the border but I think there are expectations that I'll stick with you till the Chinese send someone to take charge." The young Russian grinned. "And I have to get this fraudulent Ford back to Tashkent. If I do not after the trick we played, I might as well not return at all."

"So don't," Chappy said. Orkovsky made no answer.

The border crossing was uneventful. The guards inspected nothing, only looked at their papers and waved them on. None the less, Wilk noted small tokens of gratitude being handed to guards on both sides. "It does not hurt to leave a tip," admitted Kasim. "Especially for those of us who will return this way soon."

The Turkoman stood gazing down the road east. Camels and horses were being started on their way into China. "We have passed what some call the Dzungarian Gate. There is much of this high country yet to traverse and a long way down into desert. No one will pay much attention to us again until we reach Wusu. No one official." He turned back to the three travelers. "It is time we all go armed."

Interview, Part Six

"And so you finally made it to China. You visited again in later years." This was clear from both the biographical notes I had and my personal knowledge of the man. "And had lengthy stays."

"Twice more. I had hoped to remain the last time, to have it my home, but the Japanese and then Mao made that impossible." The slight hint of an old enmity, a remnant of anger, behind those words slipped away as Wilkins continued. "To be sure, I have made business trips there since the war, to Hong Kong, to Taiwan. To Macao." There was almost a sigh when he named that last city.

"And unofficial trips into Communist China, it is said."

"There were things I needed to know yet. It was dangerous to return in Forty-nine, but I did. I did, that one last time."

Rita raised her eyes to me and gave me the slightest shake of her head. It was a warning to change subjects. But it would be hard to avoid speaking of China and the wife he had lost there, the wife John Wilkins had searched for after the war. He had always been reticent about speaking of her, as long as I had known him.

"It was a long way from the border to civilization in Nineteen Nineteen, wasn't it?" I asked.

A smile. "In all directions. You can't get away from it now!"

16.

Armed they did go. Every traveler carried a gun. Some carried two. Chappy and Wilk wore their Smith and Wessons, and Orkovsky his Nagant revolver. Both were somewhat popular choices with others in the caravan. There was a scattering of Webley handguns as well. Kasim had one.

"Heavy," he admitted, "and it kicks worse than a camel! You will find more of them being offered for sale as you travel east. They are popular in China." Wilk rode beside him or Axana now and then, on a borrowed horse that obviously disliked him. Or perhaps it only considered him a nuisance, and to be ignored.

"But it is our tamest animal," the girl assured him, and then giggled. "Maybe Kolya should give you lessons." Orkovsky had demonstrated that he rode very well. But he chose not to and usually rode in the lorry, with the Winchester close beside him.

He took the protection of their airplanes seriously. Wilk honestly did not care whether they ever made it to the Chinese authorities, nor whether he did, for that matter. He would as soon travel the caravan routes the rest of his life, he sometimes thought. What awaited him at home, anyway? What *was* home?

Even better was riding this road beside Axana. The bargain she had made was an easy one; she was to teach him Mandarin in the mornings and he must teach her French in the afternoons. So they spent much time in each others company, conversing in those languages as best they could. Kasim gave the two a thoughtful look from time to time. Jagatai's looks were not so thoughtful. Glares would describe them better.

Down they went, into the deserts, and on to the outpost town of Wusu. Wilk was perhaps a bit disappointed that the architecture looked little different from that in the villages on the other side the border. There was no knowledge of him and his companions, nor their mission there, but the Chinese officials looked over their papers and passed them on. There was a perfunctory inspection of the various traders' goods, some bribes proffered and accepted, and those too were passed on. It was too soon for any to fall out of their company. That would come.

The Packard did occasionally fall out of the caravan. So did the other two motor vehicles, the one a Model T Ford, the other a decrepit Renault. There might be breakdowns but usually it was a matter of flat tires. When one needed to halt, all three did; they could hurry to catch up later.

"It's only right we 'elp each other out," opined Chappy. "None of us would want t' be stuck out 'ere if there's bandits about."

For some reason, Kasim always stopped with them as well, while Axana and Jagatai and the camels traveled on with the rest of the company.

They had just crossed a second river since departing Wusu when a spoke broke in one of the Ford's wheels. They were not much in the way of rivers but Wilk had been surprised to see any in what he expected to be desert. What he had expected were the many rocks, dull reds and ochers, along the ways. One of these was the culprit. Or perhaps the driver was for not missing it.

It was only a matter of putting on one of the spares but it would stop them for an hour or so. "It can be repaired in Tihwa," said its driver, in his broken Russian. "And we may not stay with this caravan beyond there."

"That is near, isn't it?" Orkovsky asked.

"It is. Another day or so. I may be able to sell everything there." The Ford seemed laden mostly with cottons, both clothing and material, and much of it printed in bright colors. "Or I might get a better price further on, or find better goods to carry back to Tashkent."

"If you go too far east, you'll be competing with British cottons," warned Kasim.

"Very true," agreed the trader, working to unloosen the broken wheel. "I shall certainly go no further than Hami."

Kasim nodded, his expression knowing. "That may be the end of my road too. Ready for us to lift?"

The Ford was not a large and heavy automobile, and it was reasonably easy for the group of men to lift the broken wheel clear of the ground. A wooden crate was slipped under its frame to hold it up until the replacement was ready.

The driver of the Renault, a small Chinese man who ever wore a voluminous duster, suddenly pointed north, babbling something in a confusing mix of Mandarin and Turkic. A handful of horsemen sat on a ridge there, watching. "Local Mongols, no doubt," commented Kasim. It seemed of no great importance to him. "Unlikely to cause trouble with this many of us down here. One truck — who could say?"

"Still, a good idea to have rifles in our hands," said the Ford driver. "Or your hands while I work."

It did seem a good idea. Wilk and Orkovsky both retrieved theirs from the Packard. Chappy was busy helping with the wheel.

Kasim held a Mosin-Nagant carbine. It was usually slung over his back. "We are as likely to be robbed by renegade troops as bandits," stated the Turkoman trader. "More so as we move east."

"Rebels out of Sinkiang, as well," muttered the man getting the wheel into position. "Or rebels out of Mongolia, for that matter. The road passes very near their border. Alright, lift again!" By the time they were ready to move forward, the riders had disappeared. Kasim rode with them on the truck seat, his horse having gone ahead with the caravan. Orkovsky chose to ride in the Ford, his Winchester ready at hand, as the seller of cottons had no traveling companions.

Neither did the driver of the Renault but he ever kept to himself. Wilk realized he did not know the man's name, nor his business.

Kasim spoke after a few minutes. "Orkovsky's words of the future have weighed on me. I may mostly bring back gold on this trip. Gold to put away somewhere against future need. Maybe in another country."

"Leave your homeland?" asked Wilk.

"We spend a great deal of time outside it already. There is Sinkiang, or we could go south to Persia or India. Kashmir is very beautiful." The Turkoman frowned at the road ahead for a few seconds. "For me, this is not such a great thing, maybe, but I worry about my daughter's future."

"Jagatai seems to worry about her, as well," commented Wilk. He had been hesitant about mentioning it.

"He does. He is a good boy and very loyal to me. And of course I do not have to be concerned about him and my Axana." Kasim leaned forward, looking across Wilk to Chappy. "But maybe I should worry about my Jagatai?" There was nothing threatening about his tone; it was more like a jest.

Wilk recognized at once what Kasim was implying. "Oh. So that's where Jagatai gets the cigarettes." The men on either side of him laughed at the comment.

Well, it was no concern of his, if Kasim didn't mind. Chappy was not much older than the Mongol lad, after all. Maybe not even as old as Wilk.

As young as Wilk was, he was certainly the most experienced of his companions. The two recognized him as their de facto leader. He knew that and knew responsibility went with it.

He shouldn't be here. He should be back in school. He should be back with his family. A family on the other side of the world.

17.

Tihwa was the capital of this province or region or whatever the Chinese government called it. For the first time, representatives of that government knew about Wilk and his mission.

"You are to be met in Hami," a minor official assured him. The man seemed thoroughly disinterested. Perhaps because there was no money to be made. It was not Axana but Kasim himself who translated for him, though Wilk could follow the exchanges in Mandarin now to some degree. He must learn the language better before reaching Hami. It would be some six-hundred kilometers to there from Tihwa; Axana could teach much in the time it took to travel the distance.

"We need petrol," he said. Kasim seemed to turn that from a request to an order for much more than just fuel. The official acquiesced to most of it, perhaps simply to be rid of them. He was the first man Wilk had glimpsed in traditional robes. Those robes were not in the best of condition, frayed and dusty, but the dark blue silk whispered of a world unknown to the young man, the China that lay ahead.

"Many ambitious bureaucrats have taken to wearing western clothes," Kasim confided as they left the dreary government offices. "Maybe most of them. You find holdouts in places such as this. Now we must see if the army is willing to honor the order he wrote for us." He held up the paper, directing the transfer of gasoline to Wilk's party.

"I suspect our original orders will prove more effective," replied the young pilot. Those had gotten them what they needed before.

As they did now. The junior officer in charge of the supply depot was not only willing but enthusiastic. "Ah, would that we had aeroplanes here." The lieutenant laughed. "If we had anyone who could fly them!"

"You could learn," Wilk told him. "My understanding is that I shall be handing these over to a flight school." That had all been, admittedly, nebulous. As was his own fate after delivering the Avros. The Chinese might or might not want to him to stay on as an instructor. He himself might or might not want to stay on.

"Perhaps I shall ask for a transfer. Lieutenant Ren, aviator. I like the sound of it!"

Kasim shook his head. "It is dangerous enough to remain on the ground, Lieutenant. But as long as we travel there we shall need some things."

Food was arranged. Kasim attempted to bargain for some ammunition, as well, only to find none that fitted the guns they carried. Wilk had noted the soldiers carried Mauser rifles. It was too bad they couldn't bargain for those! They quite outclassed the ancient Martini-Henry he still carried.

Here at Tihwa, some joined the caravan, some left to return across the border, some dawdled to do business, some hurried on to do business elsewhere. The way east was not the same when Wilk again took to the road. The road was better, wider, and there were clear signs of wheeled traffic.

"There are mining operations off a little to the north," explained Kasim, waving an arm toward the brown haze that lay along the horizon. "They extract some sort of salts. I know little of such things but I do know their trucks travel this road."

So they traveled on, at no more than the speed of Kasim's camels, and those of the other traders who traveled with the company. Wilk did not mind, for he enjoyed riding beside Axana and felt sure she enjoyed riding by him. She undoubtedly shirked her duties as camel-driver but Kasim said not a word about it.

"Autumn comes soon," she said to Wilk. "*Automne*, no?" He nodded an assent. His thoughts were not on language lessons. "Father will want to be on the road back to Tashkent. It would not do to travel in winter."

The man had mentioned he might go no further than Hami. And Wilk would journey beyond that city, far beyond it. All the way home, eventually, wouldn't he? "You have a home in Tashkent?"

"No — well, yes, we live with my Uncle Adrik when we are there.

But it is not our house. Do you have a house, Loup?"

"My family has two houses. One in the city, one in the country. The one in the country is much larger."

"Oh." She considered this in silence for a moment. Maybe Axana hadn't known his family was prosperous. "I do not know any cities in Poland. Was it a big city? As big as Tashkent?"

"It is named Danzig and I'm not really sure how the two compare. It was big enough and, like Tashkent, a center of trade. But a seaport."

Axana sighed. "I've never seen the sea. Except the Caspian!"

"The Baltic is no larger, but it connects to the ocean and to the world."

"Yes, the Caspian is really just a big lake. You can only go around and around in it."

"That's all most people ever do anyway," said Wilk. Like Axana and her father, passing back and forth on this road. Both remained silent for a while, riding side by side. "Danzig was not a Polish city when I grew up. It was part of Germany." It might still be. There had been little news recently of such things.

"You miss it?"

"Not as much as I might have thought." It was so. Perhaps the war was to blame for that. All the homesickness had gone out him during the years of fighting. "But I would not mind smelling the salt air again, nor hearing the gulls." Memories came back, one after another, becoming a rush of images. "Or smelling the hay at our country home or picking apples or sitting by the piano in the evening while my mother played."

"My mother is dead." Axana reported this in a quite matter of fact manner. "We do grow apples in Turkestan. You could live there, you know."

"The Russians might not permit it." And his father certainly expected him to come back and take up the family business. Not that his sisters and their sensible husbands couldn't handle things without him. "But I did want to go back and get to know the place better sometime."

"Don't wait too long to do it. Would you kiss me, Loup?" she asked of a sudden.

"Would your father not disapprove?" And maybe more than disapprove, Wilk warned himself.

"Oh, he doesn't dare kill you." She giggled. "Not yet."

That was good to know. He leaned over from his saddle, intending to give her a reasonably chaste kiss on the cheek. Axana had other ideas. Her arm went around him, pulling him to her lips. For a moment, Wilk feared he would tumble headfirst from his mount.

That fear flew swiftly away and he allowed himself to enjoy the moment. None the less, there were strong misgivings. He chose to make light of it as they parted. "Anyone at a distance might think I was kissing a boy," he said.

Axana wore the same dun-colored baggy pants and high boots as most of the other riders, but topped off with an at least slightly incongruous blue woolen jersey. At least her long hair was not stuffed into a turban today, but pulled back and tied. It was dark with just a touch of a chestnut-red to it. From the neck up she looked very much a girl.

"Are you going to tell me how to dress, Loup?" she demanded. "You are not my father! Anyway, George Sand wore men's clothes and she was a great writer."

"That is true," lied Wilk. He had never read any Sand but did know she sometimes dressed as a man.

"You will have to kiss me again, sometime," Axana told him. "But now, let us practice our French."

Interview, Part Seven

"Axana became a novelist herself, writing in French, of course. And, as her idol, she chose to write under a man's name."

"Would I recognize it?"

"Perhaps, but it is not mine to reveal." He gazed out the window. The city of Paris lay below us. "We met again, later."

He said no more. It would be best not to pursue the subject of Axana for now. Axana who? Wilkins had mentioned no family name. "Your family lived near Gdansk, then?"

"Yes. Our business was in what became the Free State of Danzig after the war, but our country home was in Poland. That became a difficulty, and more so when the Nazis took over the city."

"Long before then, the Russians invaded your homeland again, with your acquaintance Tukhachevsky leading them."

"That came while I was in China. It was a good thing I had decided to leave the Reds." A faint smile came and went. "I might have even been tempted to go and fight with Pilsudski, despite my dislike for the man."

"But you did serve him later, did you not?"

"I served the government for a while. Not after the Sanacja took power and Pilsudski became a dictator. I joined the opposition movement."

"Paderewski headed that, right? You knew him?"

"I did. The maestro was leader more in name than fact, at least toward the end." Wilkin paused a few seconds, remembering perhaps, before adding, "I did visit his home."

"In Switzerland."

"And in California."

A woman's voice announced the need to fasten our seat-belts as the Seven-Forty-Seven descended to a landing.

18.

The seller of cottons and his Ford Model T had gone no further than Tihwa, but the Renault journeyed on with them and they were joined by a pair of larger trucks. These held to the speed of the caravan though they could have sped ahead.

Sped, relatively speaking. No one traveled quickly on this road. The trucks were laden with hides, both of sheep and cattle. "We take all way nearest rail-head," reported one driver in somewhat barbarous English. To each other they spoke an equally barbarous Chinese dialect, according to Axana. Wilk was unable to understand much of it.

He did, however, roll out a map and look it over. It was a new chart obtained in Tihwa. Unfortunately, new only to him and his companions, for it had been printed nearly two decades prior and the railways shown were surely not up to date. Wilk and Chappy were happy to have any map with Western lettering on it, as it was difficult to puzzle out the Cyrillic on the map Orkovsky carried.

Orkovsky now compared the two. "Down at Sian, it would appear. Your map has it as Sian Fu."

Wilk nodded. "On the Hwang Ho. Or no, a tributary."

"Do y' reckon we'll be goin' there?" asked Chappy.

"It's possible. We're heading that general direction, anyway."

They saw plenty enough cattle with their hides still on as they traveled. Sheep, as well, though not so predominant as earlier in the journey. Sometimes these were being driven along the road. Sometimes they grazed in the lands on either side. They did not look like good lands for raising anything to Wilk, yet people prospered here.

Their way rose some too, growing more mountainous after a town named Kitai to him. Wilk rose one morning to frost. It was September now, wasn't it? And they were at a higher altitude. Kasim certainly would want to head back to Turkestan soon.

Unless he wintered in this country. Wilk rather liked the idea of being able to see Axana all through the seasons of cold. And maybe the seasons beyond — maybe he would wish to head back to Turkestan himself. Why not?

There came a meeting of roads. "We can turn south here, across the highlands to join the Silk Road out of Sinkiang," Kasim informed them. "Or continue as before and turn further on. We save some days by turning now. You may choose; I will stay with you on either road."

"It does not look like that much of a saving," said Orkovsky, peering at his map. "And won't traveling across those mountains slow us?" He peered now at the low range flanking them on the right. To some degree, they were already climbing into it.

Kasim only shrugged. "Perhaps so. We travel over mountains either way."

Wilk could see this. Of course, they expected him to decide. "Let's turn now," he said. He was fairly certain that was what Kasim desired. They owed Kasim.

The two large trucks turned with them. The Renault did not. The same was true of those on horseback or camel; some went each way. "Some of those who go the other way may intend to turn north into Mongolia," explained Kasim. "Hami lies very close to the border."

"And you intend to turn back there," spoke Orkovsky.

"So it is."

"If a pilot is waiting, I may be able to as well. Or another truck, for that matter."

It was at dusk on that first day after turning that one of the other travelers rode up to Kasim and conferred for a few minutes. "We are being spied upon," he reported. "Horsemen have come and gone on the ridges above us. We will want to keep our rifles close."

Wilk was, as ever, wearing his revolver. He had taken to carrying it on his left side, butt forward, though most of his comrades chose to wear their weapons on their right.

"Would they attack in the night?" asked Orkovsky. "Should more men remain on guard?"

"Yes and yes," replied the Turkoman, "though if we do the latter the

77

first might not happen. They would wish to take us unawares sometime."

"But they do not know we have spotted them," said Wilk, and then chuckled. "Or Suliman has spotted them."

"Most true. And we must not let them know." Kasim went off to confer with other travelers. They recognized him as a man knowledgeable of these ways through the wastes.

"I should ride in the truck tomorrow," announced Wilk. "Or maybe one of the Chinese trucks." He would be of help to no one on horseback and it might be a good idea to have someone with a rifle riding in each of the three motor vehicles. He would mention this to Kasim.

What were those lurking riders after? Nothing but what they could get, horses and camels and whatever they might chance to be carrying? Or did they know of Kasim's goods or even of the airplanes?

No, no. The hides and the trucks they filled. Those were obvious. Those would attract brigands. Not that those brigands would balk at taking anything else they might find, nor mind murdering them all while at it.

The night proved uneventful. All doubted the day would be the same. Wilk was awakened well before dawn. "Are you a good shot, Wilk?" whispered Kasim, squatting beside him in the dark.

There was no need to be modest. "I am." An excellent shot, some might say, but there was no need to boast either.

The Turkoman accepted this without question. "Then you and I need go hunting. Hmm, and Axana too. Bring your rifle."

In a few minutes the trio had saddled horses and ridden away from camp. Whatever plan Kasim had, it was to be assumed he had informed the others. "There is a narrow place ahead that is a likely spot for an ambush," he said, after a while. Wilk could barely make out the man's grim smile by the light of the stars. "But they no longer have the element of surprise."

"We do," added Axana. Both carried rifles. Wilk could not make out what sort they were in the darkness, but Kasim's did not appear to be his usual short carbine. He carried the Martini-Henry himself. Yes, its rate of fire was relatively slow but it was accurate and he had familiarized himself with the gun.

"Loup grew up on a great country estate and shot peasants," Axana confided to her father. Wilk was not certain whether that was a joke.

"A small country estate," he corrected her. "And most of my marksmanship I learned in the army." He believed it had served him well as a pilot. The ability to find and accurately attack a target was more important than any flying skills.

It was evident Kasim intended to ambush the ambushers. Wilk suspected he had included his daughter to keep her out of the line of fire — and, if things went wrong, to escape with her. But then she might be a good shot too.

"The likely spot is a little ahead," announced Kasim after a few minutes riding through the hills. "The bandits would like their victims to string out some in the narrow place so they can attack the center and separate the ends."

That sounded reasonable. "But not strung out too much," responded Wilk. "They would want to keep their targets close together, close enough to keep them all under observation and control."

Kasim's look might have held a restrained admiration. "Even so. Or they may be idiots who have thought none of this through. Of course, they would prefer to intimidate rather than actually shoot. That might damage valuable goods!" He allowed a quick chuckle for his jest and spoke seriously again. "I suggested our fellows leave large gaps. And that the trucks be scattered through the caravan rather than all together."

None of that might matter. There would be attackers swooping down from above, however prepared they might be, and quite probably sharpshooters stationed above them.

Those they must deal with first. He could see his comrades now by the light of a chilly dawn and could see both carried long bolt-action infantry rifles. Not Mosin-Nagants nor Mausers, that he could tell.

WILK

"Enfields?" he hazarded.

Axana nodded. "You have fired one?"

"No, but plenty have been fired at me."

Kasim had binoculars trained on the area ahead. He nodded with some satisfaction. "Just where I expected. We must go carefully now. Hmm, we can ride a little further."

The riding was not difficult, or not as difficult as Wilk had feared. But then, those bandits would prefer an easy route to their ambush.

"Do you know how many?" he asked. Wilk whispered though he doubted it was necessary.

"No more than twenty." This was surely a guess. "We need to find the two or three they may have hidden above." Kasim again scanned with his glasses and then dismounted. Axana and Wilk also dropped to the hard rocky ground.

Below, Wilk could see the front end of their caravan approaching, a horseman leading a line of camels. The rest of the travelers had indeed spread themselves out. That would make it more difficult for the bandits to choose a time and place to attack.

But perhaps make defense more difficult. There were often trade-offs in tactics.

"There's one," breathed Axana, pointing.

"You take him, Wilk," said Kasim. "If we don't locate any others, Axana and I will fire on the main group." Those, too, could be seen — more than a dozen mounted men waiting in the rocks a little above the road, their horses stamping with impatience and anticipation.

The sniper was preparing for a shot. Wilk could see that. The signal for an attack? He glanced again toward the mounted men. One who was surely their leader had raised a hand. "I'm taking out the boss," he suddenly announced and turned his Martini toward the man. A longer shot than any he had practiced with this rifle. The crack of the discharge echoed from the rocky slopes. His target slowly slumped, folded, slid from his saddle.

He had already levered out the spent cartridge and loaded another.

"'Ere they come!" he could hear Chappy call out below. Axana and Kasim began firing. He paid no attention to whether they hit anyone. Wilk was searching for the other hidden shooters. The one they had spotted before was looking about, trying to locate them, and leaving himself open. Wilk could only shake his head at the fool before sending a bullet toward him. The man spun around and toppled from his perch.

"There's another one," Axana yelled. She released a round toward a man scrabbling up the hillside at some distance beyond the one Wilk had taken out. It was a very long shot and one anybody would have been likely to miss. Her target disappeared over a low ridge.

The bandits had made only one halfhearted feint toward the caravan before they too turned and ran. "They prefer an easy thing," remarked Kasim. "Too bad we couldn't get any of their horses."

"They did leave a body," Axana said, peering downward. "The one Loup shot."

"I'm going to go check the other one I hit," Wilk announced. "Don't leave without me."

19.

One of the camel drivers had been slightly wounded. Worse, one of the camels was badly wounded and had to be put down and quickly butchered.

"I'm sure we wounded some of those bandits before they turned tail," claimed Chappy.

"My daughter and I may have wounded some as well," Kasim replied. "But our Wilk slew two of them. And he got a horse out of it."

The sniper's pony had been tied near where he fell. There was little of interest in the bags it carried. Of more interest were the things Wilk found with the body, and that he found he had no qualms about plundering it. A rifle, of course. No handgun but a short curved sword. Some ammunition. Tobacco. A few copper coins. Chinese, they appeared to be. The ragged clothes he left, though they might have fit him.

"By rights, you should get whatever was on the body of the other man too," declared Axana.

"I don't know if I want anything. The horse I give to you, Kasim. I do want to look over this rifle. I've never seen one like it."

"Rolling-block," proclaimed one of the Mongol horse-traders who had joined their caravan. "Good rifle."

It said 'Remington' on it. Wilk knew nothing of it otherwise. If the bandits' leader had carried a rifle, it had gone with his horse. However, there had been a revolver. It had been in his hand when Wilk took his shot and had fallen beside the body.

Otherwise, the man had not carried much more than the sniper. The pouch on his belt had held a small pipe. Kasim sniffed at it. "Opium," he whispered and made no further comment.

Wilk had seen no evidence of the opium Kasim supposedly smuggled. He wondered if it were no more than a tale. They left the body lying where it fell and traveled on. Someone relieved it of jacket and boots.

At their camp that evening, Wilk sat down and carefully disassembled the Remington. He was intrigued by the ingenious mechanism of the 'rolling block.' Yes, it was outmoded, a single-shot relic of the previous century — as was the rifle that had served him so well this day. He reassembled it just as carefully.

"You could be a fine gunsmith," commented Kasim, who had sat watching and smoking. "There is always money in guns."

Wilk looked up and smiled. "In smuggling them?"

"Perhaps." Both laughed.

"I've always been interested in guns and their mechanisms," Wilk went on. "As I told you, I learned to shoot well in the military but I was not a newcomer to firearms." He laid the Remington aside. "I think I will not want to keep this one. Can you find someone who needs it?"

Kasim nodded. Wilk did not care whether he gave it away or sold it. "Perhaps you would like to look at the pistol too?" He held out the revolver, sheathed in a well-tooled leather holster.

Wilk took it, looked it over. "French." He held it up, tested its balance. It had a good feel to it. "How — oh." The cylinder swung out of the frame for loading. "Hmm, I think I would have liked it better if it loaded on the other side."

"I could understand you wanting to load with your left hand. You are better with it than most right handed men. I have noticed this." Kasim chuckled. "The Lebel was designed for normal men."

"I like it. This I might keep." He peered into the cylinder and the barrel. "Rather small caliber." Wilk looked up. "Have you any idea whether cartridges are available?"

Kasim only shrugged. "Our dead bandit must have been able to find them."

"Indeed. Maybe — yes, maybe this would be a better gun for someone smaller. Axana perhaps."

"I do not want my daughter carrying a revolver. Nor any gun, Wilk." The trader sighed. "This is no life for her."

Wilk agreed but did not say so. Kasim's family was not his business.

"I'll hang onto it then." He slipped it back into its holster. "I may not need any rifles once I make my delivery."

"Yes, your delivery." Kasim seemed to ponder something and then reach a decision. "Chappy!" he called. "It is time I remove my goods from your truck."

The Englishman had been somewhere nearby. Jagatai, it appeared, had been somewhere nearby with him. He gave Wilk a glance. "Lettin' 'im in on it?"

"It's only fair. But we needn't let Orkovsky know about any of this, eh?"

"Right-o." Chappy climbed onto the truck bed and began removing items from one of the Avro fuselages. Odds and ends had been stuffed in there from the time they had begun this trip. "Ah. 'Ere we are." He pulled out a wooden box, perhaps half a meter long, then another. Four in all. He handed them down to Kasim and Jagatai.

"We've been carrying your goods?" asked Wilk. He had to admit he was more amused than bothered. Still — the man had placed him in a certain amount of danger.

"I admit it is one reason I first befriended you." Kasim laughed. "The main reason! I knew you would pass through all inspections without a problem."

Wilk had to laugh as well. "I should expect such from you, my friend. But not from Mister Chapman." He scowled at the man, or attempted to.

"It seemed like a good idea," said Chappy. "We 'elp 'im and 'e 'elps us."

"But without asking me."

"Well, sir, you would've said no, wouldn't you?"

Of course he would have. Wilk shrugged and made no reply.

"Chappy, could you and Jagatai carry those over to my camp and keep an eye on them till I get there? I need to speak with Wilk, I think."

"Sure. Come on, Jag." Each took a box under either arm and walked away. Wilk wondered if the young Mongol even knew what they contained.

Kasim stood eyeing the airplanes. "Imagine if you could fly across borders with my merchandise. I could make you a partner, Wilk. Axana would like that."

"Not in these airplanes. They are not mine." The whole idea was preposterous but Wilk decided to lead with this argument.

"But who does own these airplanes? Not the Chinese government. You've never handed them over. The Russians? They're not going to come looking for them."

"That would be a dirty trick to play on Kolya."

"He is welcome to remain too. Just not with Axana!"

Wilk found that funny. "We might as well steal the lorry too, then."

"The Packard-that-is-a-Ford? Or is it the other way around? You could get good money for it. Ah, but it would be unkind to our Russian friend, wouldn't it? Best to send him home. He'll be happier there."

That was undoubtedly true. "But where would I be happy?" asked Wilk, and at once regretted saying it aloud. Yet it had been the question on his mind these past weeks. Longer than that. Maybe as far back as the end of the war.

"I would hope you could be happy here. Perhaps with Axana." Kasim sighed deeply and perhaps more melodramatically than was called for. "Axana has refused every man, every offer of marriage — and I do not blame her. Not one was good enough! But a man such as you I would be proud to call my son."

Wilk found no words for an answer. "Think on this, Wilk," said the Turkoman trader, and followed Jagatai and Chappy into the night.

20.

He was torn. A part of Wilk was all too willing to remain in this land, remain with Axana. He loved the girl, didn't he?

A part told him he should travel on. All the way to his home on the other side of the world? He knew not whether anything he desired waited there. Poland was as foreign a land, it seemed, as China.

Ah, but he had pledged to deliver these airplanes. That road yet lay long before Wilk. Let him first fulfill his duty and what would follow would follow. He knew that was no answer, that he was avoiding a decision. So it must be.

They reached the road out of Sinkiang and again turned eastward. Hami was near. Maybe there would be answers there. The two hide trucks left them and their camel-pace, going ahead. A cool wind from the northeast whispered of the changing season.

Then the town of Hami lay before them. Many were camped about it, some in tents or wagons, others sleeping in the open as Wilk and his companions had all the way from Turkestan. "We'll do some business here, tonight, I am sure," spoke Kasim, "and go into Hami tomorrow for more."

Kasim had already sold some part of his goods, and purchased others. Wilk understood that he would try to unburden himself of those here and return home with as light a load as practical. Return home with Axana. The time had come for parting.

There was business done throughout the campgrounds that night. Wilk was fairly certain the boxes of opium had been handed over. Kasim would do a more ordinary sort of trading tomorrow. All those here would and some, like Kasim, would turn back and some would go forward.

That night, also, Wilk shaved his beard, leaving only a dark mustache. Chappy decided to do the same but after giving the wispy growth on his upper lip a good look in their little metal mirror, chose to take it off too.

"I'll shave when I get back to Russia," claimed Orkovsky, stroking his full whiskers. "Or maybe never."

"You look like a true Bolshevik," was Chappy's comment. Wilk chose to comment not at all.

The next morning they entered the city. There was only perfunctory checking of most papers but Orkovsky wanted to report to the authorities at once. "There might be a pilot here," said the Russian. He sounded hopeful.

There was not. "There will be orders in Ansi," a bureaucrat in a dark, ill-fitting suit assured them. He also promised to telegraph ahead of their arrival.

"I doubt he has any idea whether they know about us in Ansi," sighed Orkovsky as they exited the shabby office. "But he will probably send a wire."

"So we travel together a little longer. I shall deliver these planes, Kolya, whether I choose to go on with them or not."

Orkovsky was quiet for a few seconds. "I thank you for that." He looked about the bustling town as they emerged into daylight. The sky was completely clear above them, and an intense blue. "I can see the attractions of remaining here, Wilk, but that is not for me. I miss Russia."

And Russian girls, thought Wilk. "We can loiter here a day or two," he said. "We can use the rest."

Orkovsky smiled. "Until Kasim and Axana leave?"

"Yes." There was no reason to explain anything more. But he did add, "I should check over the Packard. Here, if I can. Definitely before you attempt to drive it back."

"Maybe I could return by the Silk Road through Sinkiang and over the high pass. I won't have any load going back."

Wilk frowned at the idea. "I don't think I would attempt it. Kasim says he will go back by the way we came. Perhaps if you hurry you can even catch up with him." Assuming they could part in Ansi.

That town lay another three-hundred kilometers south. It would take some time to reach it. Wilk doubted they would hold to the speed of camels any longer. There was no need. The roads were better and there was a fair amount of motor traffic. It was almost civilized here.

Chappy waited at the lorry and Axana waited with him. "We must go to the markets, Loup," she proclaimed. "There are many things to buy here."

"I'll stay with the truck," offered Orkovsky.

Chappy recognized that left him free. "Are we buyin' or sellin'?" he asked, falling in with them.

"Maybe both," Wilk replied. "What do we have we can part with? I could use some pocket money." Orkovsky had been controlling the purse strings. That purse would disappear when he left.

"One of the rifles, maybe? Or y'r pistol, seein' as y' 'ave a new one."

Wilk liked the 'new one.' It was tighter and better finished than the Smith and Wesson. The Russian weapon seemed crude in comparison. He should see if he could find the eight millimeter ammunition the Modele 1892 used.

So Chappy fetched one of the Russian revolvers, and the Martini-Henry as well. They wore no weapons on their persons — only police and soldiers did so within the bounds of Hami. Wilk decided he should devise a way to carry the French revolver inconspicuously. Maybe inside his pants waist somewhere, or in a shoulder holster.

Wilk considered also selling the sword he had taken from the dead bandit. He had carried the blade with him since obtaining it. He had even worn it occasionally, though he had felt a bit silly with it hanging on his belt. And it did get in the way of his holster — he had not decided on a practical arrangement for carrying both weapons. No, the sword might be useful sometime and it was a bit of a souvenir. He left it in the truck.

There were certainly weapons for sale here. An assortment, long and short, rifles, shotguns. Even some muzzle-loaders — that would be one way to get around the problem of finding proper ammunition. There were many other things available too, most of them useful. "We may need some warmer clothes, Chappy," said Wilk.

"Or more blankets," the Englishman replied.

"Let my father tend to that," Axana told them. "He knows people."

Indeed he does, Wilk thought. Ah. "Here are cartridges for the pistol," he said. Haggling and bartering — mostly managed by Chappy — followed, ending with both the Smith and Wesson and the Martini-Henry remaining with the dealer, and Wilk and Chappy walking away with ammunition for both their revolvers and a few coins.

"Did we get a good deal?" Wilk whispered to Axana as they ambled on.

"As good as could be expected. Now let us visit the book sellers!"

Those book sellers knew Axana. "She buy here since little girl," reported one old woman with an assortment of tattered novels spread before her in a little booth. They were in many languages, as were those of the handful of other nearby book merchants they visited.

A few, to be sure, were in Chinese — printed in the Western alphabet. "I should learn to read Mandarin," he mused. "It might help me speak it."

Axana looked the volumes over. "Would you prefer one on gardening or the principles of Marxism?" she asked.

"Gardening. I'm quite done with the Reds! But maybe we should pass those up for now. Are you seeking more French novels?"

"Perhaps. Maybe I should read Polish novels." She giggled. "But in French."

Wilk perused the book seller's offerings. "Ah, there's Conrad. He's Polish, but he writes in English."

"I can read English. Some. Is he any good?"

Wilk admitted he did not care for the man's writing, as he handed the novel to her. He was surprised to see Axana pull out a pair of over-sized, steel-rimmed spectacles and perch them on her aquiline nose. "I need these to read," she announced, perhaps with a note of defensive-ness.

"So what languages do you read?" he asked.

"Oh, Russian, of course, but I do not like Russian novels. So dreary!"

"There are dreary French novels," Wilk told her. "Avoid Flaubert."

Axana nodded, a bit absentmindedly, as she leafed through *Nostromo*. "I think not," she said, replacing it on the table. "I do read English. Better than French, maybe." A slight smile, maybe a little sad, followed. "I would like to be able to read the languages of my home-land. Of my ancestors. But I have seen only Russian translations of the old stories."

"Then maybe you should write them down yourself," Wilk suggested.

"Maybe so. Who do you think I would like, Loup? Pick out a book for me!"

"Very well." He looked over the selection before pulling out a decid-edly tattered specimen. "Have you read Stendahl?"

A frown of thought. "No. It sounds like a German name."

"Yet he was French. You might like this." He handed her the copy of *La Chartreuse de Parme*.

Axana read all the first page and part of the second before closing the book. "Yes, I want this one. And now, pick one *you* especially like." She waved a hand toward the books stacked around them. "I want to read your favorite book!"

Wilk's own preferences turned more to adventure stories. Dumas? No. Maybe something in English — yes. He pulled out Kipling's *Kim*, in rather good shape. "Maybe not my favorite but I do like it." Or did like it, as a teen, before the war. How would it strike him now?

Ha, he was living a Kipling story, wasn't he? He would never need read another.

Three wandered on through the markets of Hami, but two were paying more attention to each other than what lay about them.

21.

She slipped under the blanket beside him. Wilk was not entirely surprised.

But he was unsure of this. In many ways, the young Pole was quite conventional, straitlaced, even. Axana's slender body pressed against his, their mouths found each other in the dark. He was less unsure then.

Their hands strayed and, eventually, slowly, began the undressing of each other. The night was cool and there was considerable undressing to accomplish. Perhaps that might make it all the better, some would say, but it seemed not so to the two young impatient lovers.

Before they came together, Axana giggled, saying, "You may think I am not a virgin but I am. Much horseback riding ruptured my, um, maidenhead years ago." She frequently used such words, words she had found only in books.

"I hope it was good for you," Wilk quipped and immediately regretted.

Axana only laughed. "Not as good as this."

Certainly not as good. But all good things end and they lay side by side again, each with his or her thoughts. Wilk was glad they had not slept within the town. They could have. They could even have demanded housing. Chappy did express a deep desire to sleep in a bed again. Wilk had decided to return to the campgrounds and the others had followed his order.

"What of your father?" he asked at last. Kasim had been banished from his mind for a time, but now he returned.

"Father probably knows. Or suspects. So long as we are discreet, it will not matter, but it would not do to publicly shame his house."

The thought of unwanted pregnancy flitted through Wilk's mind. No point in worrying about that at the moment. "I would never wish to shame Kasim. Nor you."

"I know that. Father knows that. You are an honorable man, my

Loup." There was a sigh, barely to be heard. "And you have done me no dishonor tonight. What Allah will think of me, I do not know."

Wilk rolled on his side to face the girl, her profile barely visible in the night. "You are Muslim?"

"In name. I am not sure what I am truly, Loup. I know I can not be an atheist like Kolya."

"Neither can I. But I can't see myself following my parents' Lutheran ways."

"Luther-anne. That is a sort of Christian, no?"

"It is. Most Poles are Catholics."

"Oh, I know of Catholics. There is a church in Ansi." He could see her face turn his way. "Why are your mother and father not Catholic?"

"Because they are of the prosperous middle class and see Catholics as superstitious peasants. That is also why I was reared more German than Polish."

"Ah, just as many take on Russian ways in Turkestan. Even Russian names."

"Like Axana?"

He was sure she snickered. "That is most rude of you, Loup. But yes, like Axana. Or Kazimir. I am called Axana but I was named Roxane at birth." There was a pause. "Never use that in public, alright?" She sounded a little anxious.

"I promise not to. But I will tonight. I think I want to make love to Roxane now."

"Fickle Loup!"

She dressed under the blanket and slipped away an hour or so later. Wilk greatly wished she could have remained with him. Till the dawn? Through the day and the next day? He fell into slumber, to awaken to the rising sun.

Orkovsky was fussing with the Packard, doing nothing important, only rearranging their cargo. "Everyone's going," he announced when Wilk approached. "Is there any reason we should dawdle?"

"Probably not. Kasim?"

"Taking off this morning. He left us some blankets." The Russian gestured toward them. "And says he will stop by to make his farewell."

Did Orkovsky have any inkling of what had happened last night? Wilk doubted it. The man had slept in the shadow of the lorry and would not have abandoned his self-imposed guard duty. And Chappy? He suspected he was making his own goodbyes to Jagatai.

Wilk surveyed the waking campground. On the road, most of these would have been up and on the go by now. "Isn't that the car that traveled part way with us?" he asked, nodding in its general direction.

Orkovsky took a look. "The Renault, yes. It arrived only a day behind us despite the longer route."

"We were held up half a day," Wilk reminded him.

"Which would not have happened if we had gone the other way. I am sure they ran into no bandits."

Wilk gave only an abstracted nod. He suspected the driver of the French automobile had hurried on his route, not bothering to travel with a caravan. Ah, but that was of no concern to him.

Chappy wandered up, looking rather disheveled. There was the start of a new beard on his face. Wilk should get back into the habit of shaving in the morning. "Ready to 'it the road again, are we?" he asked.

"We might as well. Once we say goodbye." With a heavy heart. Wilk wasn't sure he knew what that meant before, but this morning his heart indeed felt like a lump of lead. From the look on Chappy's face, he might have his own lump.

"Here comes Kasim," said Orkovsky. "Alone."

"So we say farewell," spoke the Turkoman as he approached. "Not for long, let us pray." His eyes were on Wilk as he said this.

"Only God can say," Wilk replied.

"It is so, but maybe you can prompt him. We shall travel with a caravan again, though we have little to carry this time. We shall not hurry." He took the hands of each in turn. "You should go say goodbye to Axana," he told Wilk. "She waits with our horses."

"I will."

WILK

At that moment, a small, balding Chinese man bustled up to them. He wore a duster over a suit in the Western style, including a tie and a high collar. He bowed and began speaking at once, "I understand we travel together again."

"So it seems, Mister Yao." ventured Orkovsky. "Your way here was uneventful?"

"Very quiet, sir. I have heard you had trouble with bandits."

"Only the bandits had trouble," Kasim assured him.

"Ah! That is good. I would not want anyone to steal my merchandise."

All four stared at him. None had the slightest idea what the man sold. He had been quite closed-mouth in all his interactions. "Farm implements," he informed them. "The finest and most modern!"

That interested Wilk. "Oh? I must see your merchandise when we get on the road, Mister Yao."

"At your service, Mister Wilk, and always happy to speak business."

"But later. I must go say goodbye to someone."

Axana did wait with the horses. Five horses and no more — that was all she and her father and Jagatai took home with them. The Mongol stood a bit apart, having his own thoughts.

There was nothing to say and everything to say. Wilk chose nothing and only embraced her. Maybe there would be time for everything later. Or maybe there would be no later. They both knew that.

"Goodbye, Roxane," he whispered in her ear, kissed her and turned away.

Within the hour they were on the road south toward Ansi, traveling on their own but falling into a sort of convoy of trucks and automobiles that had formed. All rode in silence for most of the morning.

"Makin' good time," Chappy remarked around noon. "We might make this Ansi town in two days, don't y' think?"

"It seems likely," replied Wilk. Orkovsky made some sort of noncommittal noise. He seemed more interested in watching the countryside go by.

94

Then the Englishman let out a long sigh. "I'll miss Jag, that I will." He pulled over a little as a motorcycle came buzzing by. "But I couldn't stay 'ere, could I?"

Wilk had no answer to that question. None at all.

Interview, Part Eight

"Had I chosen to stay then, I am sure Chappy would have too. For a while. I am also sure he would have left in time and wandered on."

"What became of Chapman?" I asked.

"Chappy never left China. He settled in Hong Kong permanently and opened a bar. I last saw him alive when I was fleeing the country in Forty-one, but I didn't make myself known to him. I've wished I could have, sometimes since." Wilkins's tone was completely matter-of-fact, the statement of a simple truth. "But I've not regretted it. It was the wise thing to do."

"He might have betrayed you to the Japanese?"

"Inadvertently. I had my daughter with me and would take no chances."

That would have been his adopted daughter, Rebecca. I already knew much about that. "You left her in Macao for the duration?" He only nodded. "And Chappy. Did the Japanese kill him?"

"No, cancer. The privations of that time of the occupation may have hastened his end." His thoughts might have drifted to his old friend for a moment. "I didn't learn of that until after the war, of course."

"This must be our driver," Rita said. A solidly built man in a gray uniform approached. "We can talk more at the hotel later. Or tomorrow before we fly on to Poland."

John Wilkins rose to his feet without aid, erect despite his ninety-five years. "Yes, we can," he said. "There's a lot more to my story."

22.

"Yao is a fraud," Wilk informed his companions. "He knows nothing of farming. My family manufactured agricultural equipment." A number of travelers had pulled aside and camped here, Yao among them. A small fee had to be paid for the privilege — a sure sign of having entered a more civilized world.

"So what's 'is game?" wondered Chappy.

Wilk could not guess. He shrugged and poured himself more coffee. Orkovsky had been able to procure fresh coffee in Hami by bullying the local officials with claims of the importance of their mission.

Orkovsky also had ideas about Mister Yao. "An agent," he said. "A saboteur. That would be my bet."

Wilk realized he knew nothing of the politics of the China they had entered. Yes, there was a power struggle of some sort between two governments, and there were a number of more or less independent warlords about. "You think he might have been involved with the bandits."

"That I would bet on too. Why else did he take the other route and then hurry to join us again?"

"Wants t' steal the airplanes?" asked Chappy.

"Or destroy them," conjectured Wilk.

Orkovsky nodded. "Exactly. Sent by Peiping, probably, in hopes of disrupting relationships between the Soviet government and that of Sun Yat-sen."

Chappy laughed. "So killin' us would work just as good."

"He'd better do it soon," commented Wilk. "We may be able to turn those planes over by tomorrow."

"I'll drink to that," said Orkovsky. "If there were anything to drink in this country."

"Y' should've said somethin' about that earlier," Chappy told him. "There was stuff available back in 'Ami."

"You could have said something about the political situation too," added Wilk.

"I doubt I know any more about that than you. I'm just a pilot, Wilk." That was not completely true, but Wilk let it pass without comment. "And you will be learning a great deal more, while I return to Russia."

"Do y' think the Chinese will give us uniforms?" asked Chappy. He sounded eager. The thought might have just come to him.

"Me, perhaps," Wilk said. "If I decide to stay."

The Englishman nodded. "I fancied the robes that Chinese fellow wore in Tihwa. Reckon I'd like t' get my 'ands on somethin' like that myself."

Orkovsky was eyeing Wilk. "I'm not sure the authorities would let you back into Russian territory. Is that what you had in mind?"

"It's one possibility," he admitted. There were too many possibilities, too many choices, ahead of him.

"Wilk could pass as a Turkoman," opined Chappy, "with his sun tan and dark hair. And with the proper papers, of course."

"True," spoke the Russian, and said no more of it.

They slept near the Packard. Orkovsky insisted they take watches though it seemed unlikely one rather small Chinese man would cause them any trouble in a crowded camp.

Too crowded, maybe. Many were curious about the airplanes and came to look at them. That, too, made Orkovsky nervous. Soon, all that could be done and over with. The Russian would part with Wilk and Chappy and the Avros he had shepherded into China. The end of a journey, the end of a tale. The Russian should write a book about it, Wilk decided, as he fell into sleep.

"'Ey! What are you up to there?"

Wilk awoke to see two burly figures confronting Chappy. Both wielded axes. One menaced the Englishman while the other climbed up onto the Packard.

He felt for his revolver and then remembered the sword. It might be preferable to shooting in the dark. Attempting to shoot. The blade lay close by, with the rest of his gear. He should have taken those fencing lessons as a boy, he told himself, as he grasped its hilt. Wilk had seen no point and turned them down. He would be willing to bet Orkovsky knew how to handle a sword.

Chappy was reaching for his revolver when the ax-man stepped forward, swung at him. The driver stumbled back, barely evading the blade, off balance, still groping for his sidearm. Wilk did not hesitate; he rushed forward, taking a two-handed swing with his own weapon. Only a warning cry from the man on the truck kept him from connecting solidly with his blade. As it was, he certainly cut the man deeply on his right arm.

The thug howled. His ax fell to the ground. By then, Chappy's gun was in his hand and Orkovsky, too, had awakened and had his own revolver out, looking about in some confusion. Both of the intruders ran for it.

"No point in going after them," said Orkovsky, coming up. "Did they do any damage?"

"Didn't 'ave time," replied Chappy and looked toward Wilk. "Thank you, sir. I think y' may 'ave saved my life there."

"Possibly," admitted the Pole. "Chinese. Dressed like it, anyway." The pair had been in what Wilk knew for more or less traditional peasant wear, blue cotton tunic and trousers. It was unlikely they actually were peasants.

A small crowd had gathered. "Thieves?" asked someone.

"Yes, thieves," agreed Wilk. "I'll take over as guard," he told Chappy.

He might as well. He couldn't sleep, not after the fray, short though it was, and there was much on his mind. Did he want to get involved in yet another war, here in China? Wouldn't it be better to seek peace? To take the chance of love and happiness that had been offered him?

Maybe he could tell Kolya to say he had died on the road. None could blame him for that. Once the planes were delivered, even if there was no one to fly them, the Russian's duty would be done. They could both return west.

WILK

Tomorrow. Wilk might need to decide tomorrow.

23.

The Renault and its driver were missing the next morning. It was said Mister Yao had headed back north, in a great hurry, sometime before dawn.

A bored soldier, a sergeant by his uniform, visited them as they prepared to move on. One look at their papers satisfied the man. He did not even ask for a bribe.

"There would have been no point in telling him about Yao," Orkovsky said when he left. "He'll be happier just reporting an attempted robbery."

So they journeyed on south to Ansi that day. Ansi was an important locus of the Silk Road, where the way split and carried travelers into Sinkiang on northern and southern routes. Some might say it was the end of the Silk Road, but perhaps that should be Yumen which lay a little further east. There, they were assured, someone awaited them.

A pilot? That was unknown. "One travels through the Jade Pass and beyond it lies Yanguan Pass and the corridor into China's heartland," the official told them, "east along the feet of the mountains." The man seemed genuinely interested in them. Perhaps they broke the tedium of his routine. He did not seem to realize they would fly from Yumen. Or attempt to fly. At any rate, Orkovsky and the truck should go no further.

Perhaps Wilk wouldn't either. He told the Russian not to introduce him to anyone nor make him known until he said so. Was he only putting off a decision that way? Wilk suspected he was but tried to banish the thought from his mind.

There were rooms that night and soldiers to guard the Packard. There were baths. Had they remained another day they might have had their laundry done but Orkovsky was eager to go on. So they took to the road, rising toward Yumen, again in the morning.

"I heard the latest news from Russia," Orkovsky said, after a time. "How current, I am not sure, but the Whites had been driven beyond the Urals."

WILK

"Would you 'ave liked t' been there fightin' with 'em?" asked Chappy.

"And miss the journey of a lifetime? Never. Yet I am happy the journey draws to its end. I shall miss the both of you."

Wilk had to chuckle. "The journey is only half over for you, my friend."

"And you've no idea how far yours goes on."

Yumen proved to be a good-sized town, part of it walled. A small automobile was parked by the road, a good distance from it, with a man in uniform leaning against it and smoking. When he spied them he stepped forward, raising a hand.

"The airplanes from Russia," he enthused. "At last!" This was in English. He must know at least a little about them.

Orkovsky was amused. "You were waiting for us?"

"We were telegraphed that you were on your way as soon as you left Ansi this morning." The man drew himself up and saluted. "Captain Shao, at your service."

"Nikolai Orkovsky." Kolya chuckled. "Lieutenant Orkovsky. I almost forgot I was still in the military!" He returned the Chinese officer's salute as he stepped out. Wilk followed him.

"This is the pilot?" The man gave Chappy an incredulous look.

"Not on y'r life," stated the Englishman, retaining his seat behind the wheel.

Orkovsky glanced toward Wilk but held his tongue. Wilk smiled despite himself. The man took him for a native of the steppes.

"That would be me," he said, stepping forward and extending a hand. "Jean Wilk. No rank." Very well. Now he had done it. But he had not really committed to anything, had he?

"Ah, good," said the captain, taking his hand. "It would have been hard to fly both back myself. One foot in each, maybe!" He gave the pair of Avros a perfunctory look and said, "Ride with me, will you? Your lorry can follow."

Wilk settled himself beside Shao in the back of the little car. "The truck and Lieutenant Orkovsky will go back to Russia now," he told him. "I should thoroughly check it over first."

"No need. There are mechanics here. You and I should make our priority getting those airplanes put back together. Avros, aren't they?" Wilk nodded. "I've flown them. There are some already at the school."

"I assume they are sent more as a gesture of friendship than to fill any pressing need," said Wilk.

"Indeed so. As are you, no? You are not Russian, I understand."

"Polish, though my papers have me as German. So I am using a French name."

"That makes complete sense. Here is the camp. There is no airfield, I am afraid, but enough open space. Some of it is almost level."

There were tents and sheds and soldiers. It was certainly recognizable as an army camp. Wilk realized he did not much like seeing one again. Not after weeks of clean open country.

"You are the only pilot they sent?" he asked Shao.

"I am. You, ah, do intend to fly one of the airplanes, don't you?"

"Yes, I suppose I do." That would be the right thing. His duty, perhaps. "But I am not at all sure how long I shall stay."

The automobile rolled to a halt. "There is another foreign instructor already at our school. An Englishman."

Wilk considered asking how far it was to that flying school but decided it didn't matter right then. Maybe it would never matter. He would fly to it or he wouldn't. Both exited the car as Chapman pulled the Packard in beside them.

The captain pointed to a nearby open shed. "We can put the planes there. Leave the truck too. I'll have a mechanic go over it for you."

Orkovsky hopped out of the Packard and Chappy drove it under the roof. "Are you interested in going into Yumen, Lieutenant?" asked the Chinese flier.

Orkovsky gave the town a looking over. "I can't say I am. I'd as soon turn around and head home as soon as possible. Winter is on the way."

Shao nodded understandingly. "Your driver goes with you?"

"No, he's mine," Wilk immediately told him. "You could call him, um, my batman." He wasn't going to abandon Chapman after bringing him this far.

"Then I will show you to your tent where you may rest and clean up. The colonel expects you for dinner." He said a few words in Mandarin to his own driver. Wilk could get the gist of it. Perhaps he shouldn't let the man know that.

Or perhaps he should keep no secrets. "We will be honored to be shown our lodging," he said, or was pretty sure he said, in Mandarin.

All three travelers followed the enlisted man — he wore what Wilk assumed were corporal's stripes — while Shao headed toward the shed. He would probably see to the unloading of airplanes and gear. "Do have our personal gear brought to us," Wilk told their guide.

"Yes, sir! Here is your tent, honored guests." The man seemed unsure whether to salute, decided not to, hurried off. Maybe to see to their belongings.

The tent was sensibly close to the shed. "Folding cots," sighed Chappy, and sprawled on one of them.

"I am pretty certain the dinner invitation doesn't extend to you, Chapman," said Orkovsky. "An officers' mess."

"No problem, sir. There's plenty enough food in our kit."

"We'll divvy all our things before I leave."

"You might as well have most of it," said Wilk. "We're not likely to need it."

Orkovsky nodded an agreement. "I'm still carrying money, including gold. Some I should leave with you."

"Not too much," Wilk warned, to Chappy's obvious disgust. "Be certain you've enough to get you back."

The corporal reappeared, leading several enlisted men bearing their belongings, as well as water. No excuse not to clean up, maybe even shave. But their clothes must be as they must be, worn and dusty from the road.

Dinner with the colonel and officers proved boring. No one spoke to them. For that matter, the Chinese officers hardly spoke to each other. The colonel was a tired-looking middle-aged man with a goatee and much golden braid. A sword hung at his side.

But the food was fairly good and the service better than Wilk had ever seen in a military setting. Or in the houses of the wealthy for that matter. It jarred a bit with the faded drab walls of a canvas tent on all sides of them.

Wilk insisted on inspecting the Packard before he would allow Orkovsky to drive away in the morning. Carefully, methodically, he went over the entire automobile before declaring it satisfactory. "Not that I couldn't have done it better," he said. "Try to have it looked at again, when you can. And be sure to check the oil!"

"I promise to return it to Tashkent in good condition," said the Russian. "And myself as well."

"You do that, Kolya." They embraced and Nikolai Orkovsky motored away into the morning.

Interview, Part Nine

"I ate here in Thirty-five," remarked John Wilkins. "I did not return to Paris for quite some time."

Rita said, "In Forty-six."

"Yes, when I brought Rebecca to her grandfather. General Peng." He gave his wife a slightly puzzled look. "We hadn't met."

"But my stepdaughter has told me of it, more than once." As she had me.

"Hmm, yes, she would. Anyway, the food was better in the Thirties."

"He thinks everything was better in the Thirties," confided Rita.

"How could it have been when I didn't have you yet, my dear?" A kiss followed that. "But we left my story somewhat earlier than that, didn't we?"

"You had just parted with Nikolai Orkovsky."

"Yes. Orkovsky overtook Kasim and Axana on the road and traveled on with them. Fortunately, he did not need the services of a mechanic and had enough spare tires!"

"So he did get back to Tashkent."

"He did. And when he got back to Tashkent he found his Yeva pregnant."

"With his child?"

"Most likely. The two had a long life together and eventually even married."

"Then you remained in touch?"

"Our paths crossed from time to time. Kolya attempted to keep a low profile but he had become labeled an expert on China."

"As were you."

Wilkins nodded amiably. "As was I."

24.

"I don't suppose that is pronounced Ow-steen."

Chappy took a look at the Austin car and then back at Wilk, before grinning. "'Avin' y'r fun with me, aren't y'?"

"Perhaps," Wilk admitted. "Shao tells me nothing is available for you to drive. You'll have to ride in an airplane with one of us."

"Well, then make sure y' put it together proper-like."

They had been working on that all the morning. Captain Shao knew little of assembling an airplane and the soldiers he requisitioned knew nothing. That mattered little; Wilk needed them primarily for heavy lifting.

It should be possible to test fly one of the Avros tomorrow, maybe both. The engines were his main concern. He had come from Russia with little in the way of spare parts and was unlikely to see more until they reached the flying school. "It is near the city you would call Canton," Shao told him. "The government rules from there for now. The true Chinese government." There was just a touch of vehemence in his voice when he stated that.

Wilk and Chappy had pulled out their map. Almost all the way to coast. "That's nearly as far as the distance we've traveled from Tashkent," said Chappy.

"As the crow flies. We wound about a good bit on the road."

"That's so. Not that I've ever seen a crow fly straight anyway."

Neither had Wilk. But here he would be flying straight, and away from Axana and her world. It was too late to turn and catch up with her and her father, was it not? Or even with Orkovsky. Better to deliver the airplanes now and not attempt to travel back in the winter. A spring would come.

And when they reached their destination, it would perhaps be as easy to go east, to America, to Europe, and reach Turkestan from that direction, as to backtrack across Asia.

They visited Yumen that evening. Shao sent the corporal with them.

WILK

The traders and merchants milling in and around the city seemed to belong to another world now. "It really feels like China for the first time," noted Chappy.

Wilk had to agree. "We left Dzungaria and entered Kansu province back a little before we reached Ansi. Kansu is long and narrow and we'll pretty much stay in it for a while, I suspect." He turned to their guide and addressed him in Mandarin. "We need clothes," he said. "Can you assist us, Corporal?"

"A tailor, sir?"

"We haven't the time." Nor the funds. "There are surely those who sell clothing, new and used, in this place."

"Maybe I c'n get me one of those silk gowns," Chappy put in.

Wilk shook his head. "Only something practical and presentable to wear while we travel on. We look like a pair of ragged nomads come down from the steppes! You may buy all the gowns you can afford when we reach our destination."

"Soldier clothes, maybe, sir? I know a good place." They followed the man to a street of shops. Most of the merchants here did wear traditional robes, most commonly black. Lanterns hung above them, paper lanterns of varied color, such as the Westerners had seen in old books. Wilk had not completely believed that sort of thing was real.

"Oh, fans!" Chappy had stopped before a display. "I've got t' 'ave me one."

"Just one," Wilk told him, laughing. "You know you'll see plenty more of them. Let's find something to wear first and see how much money we have left." He suspected prices would be better here than they had been in Hami. There was more competition, more goods available.

He looked over a table of footwear. "Boots can wait. We won't be walking much for a while."

"Thank God for that," muttered Chappy.

The shop to which the corporal led them did much business in enlisted men's uniforms, in various states of wear. Those were perhaps the last thing Wilk and Chappy would wish to wear. "Say," the Englishman said, pointing out a stack of brown apparel, "those are British." His eyes went to the next pile. "And those — hmm, don't know."

"Austrian," said Wilk. "Who could guess how they ended up here?" He looked them over. "The jacket could fit me. Or you." He and Chappy were not too different in size — especially now that months of travel had made both lean. "Warm jackets are what we need most. It will be cold flying, I fear."

"And a good jacket will 'ide a shabby shirt. We've plenty enough of those!"

They returned to their tent with jackets and trousers for both, in gray. They would do and did not speak particularly of one nation or another, especially after they cut off any decorative details with a razor. The corporal had helped them with the bargaining. Wilk gave the man a tip, of course. The merchant might well have done the same.

And, to be sure, Chappy got his fan, red and yellow silk printed with dragons.

The first Avro flew the next morning, with Wilk at the controls. He did not completely like the sound of the engine and tinkered with it through the afternoon while Shao and his crew finished putting the other plane together. They required only occasional supervision. Shao took it up himself before dark and proclaimed it ready for travel. Wilk told himself to check it over thoroughly.

"We shall start tomorrow," announced the Captain, "but only fly as far as Suchow. It is no more than a couple hours away."

A test flight. That was sensible. He would check both machines anyway.

That he did before retiring, going over both thoroughly and meticulously. Then he took each up in turn as soon as it was light. "You can stow your gear in that one," he told Chappy, waving toward the machine he had flown into Tashkent. He might as well stick with the familiar.

"I'll put y'rs in too. Worked 'ard enough, y' 'ave, Wilk, and there's lots more to come." The Pole nodded acquiescence. He could use a breather.

It was not a long one. Shao appeared at the mid-morning. He had very much dressed the part of pilot, with leather helmet and leather jacket with shearling collar, and even breeches and high boots. The captain looked quite smart and a little ridiculous.

An automatic pistol hung at his waist. Wilk was fairly certain it was a Colt though a flap covered most of it. He and Chappy wore their own revolvers. As far as helmets went, they had none, but wrapped scarves about their heads.

A few minutes later, goggles covered their eyes and they taxied across the field outside Yumen and winged eastward. There was high ground to pass over ahead. For that matter, they were already rather high up.

Wilk knew there would be more mountainous terrain to cross a few days ahead, maybe even higher than here, and then they would descend into China proper, the China of story, not these sun-baked western lands.

They reached Suchow in time for lunch.

25.

He glimpsed it, distant, off to their left. It was the afternoon of their second day.

Wilk turned to get Chappy's attention, pointed toward it. He could see the man's astonishment, read the words his lips formed. *The Great Wall.*

They would cross it eventually, twice at least. There were also mountain walls yet to cross. The biplanes dropped to a landing at Kanchow shortly after. Shao was keeping their flights short so far.

"We cross a high gap tomorrow," the captain informed them. "If we make good time, we could attempt to press on as far as Lanchow."

"Will we see the Great Wall again?" asked Chappy. It was not visible from their landing field.

"We will, and closer up," he was assured. "Let's see what sort of lodging is available." The Chinese aviator stopped and looked at their airplanes. "I must make sure a guard is posted on these. There are military leaders along the way who claim allegiance to the Republic but would not mind appropriating a pair of airplanes for their own use. Also, there are those both in Canton and Peiping who do not want to see good relations between China and the Red leaders."

"We already know of those," answered Wilk and proceeded to tell him the tale of Mister Yao, as they walked toward the military headquarters.

"Agricultural implements, eh? I should probably inform someone of your spy, though he has undoubtedly changed name and story by now."

"So we assumed. He should choose to sell something he knows about next time." Wilk chuckled. "The man did have a vague idea of a combine's use but not really how it worked."

The room offered them there was so filthy they chose to sleep in the shelter of the Avros' wings. Shao saw to their refueling early and Wilk checked over the engines. Then the captain spread a chart on one of the lower wings. "We continue to follow the road through the mountains, here." His finger traced the route.

"One of the men 'ere called that the Wushao Pass," volunteered Chappy.

"It is high, whatever one names it. Then we follow the way down past Liangchow. Or stop there, if need be."

"There is a river by Lanchow?" asked Wilk, trying to make out the printing in the dim dawn light.

"The Hwang Ho itself flows by Lanchow, looping north, and we will cross it just before we reach the city. But we will not see the river again. Our way lies south. Exactly which way south I have not quite decided."

"The flying looks easier to the north," Wilk pointed out. "We could avoid a lot of mountainous country."

"Our government does not control that area. We would not stand a chance of getting through." He pointed to an area almost due south of Lanchow. "We could follow the roads right down to Chungking before turning toward Canton. There's some rugged country that way. Or," he said, moving his finger up and to the right, "we could fly to Sian and chance crossing the highlands there."

"Oh, that's where our boys with the 'ides were 'eadin', isn't it?" said Chappy.

"So we guessed. To pick up the railroad there."

"Yes, that would be the nearest railway. The political situation might not be as good that way."

"Might not?" The captain could only smile and shrug. "Very well," Wilk continued, "I'm for going through Sian. I don't like the looks of all those mountains down there in, um, Szechwan."

"We've seen far too many mountains already," added Chappy.

"And I'm not sure I trust those engines to carry us across more of them."

"And I am inclined to defer to you on such things," said Captain Shao, folding his map. "Sian it will be, unless we hear something to change our minds in Lanchow. Let's be on our way."

The Avros labored for height, again approaching their altitude limits. It would not do to tax the Gnome rotaries much more. But they passed through the long gap, uncomfortably close to the ground at times. Traffic of other sorts shared the way, camels, horses, trucks, passing along the road below.

A group of men by the road, seated. Waiting for someone or simply resting? Wilk saw one rise, tiny at this distance. Pointing their way? The others came to their feet as well — and raised rifles. He at once banked off to the left, as bullets came whistling past.

Was Shao alright? What was the idiot doing? The Chinese pilot maintained his course almost over the shooters. Suddenly, an explosion below. The men scattered. Most of them. At least two lay on the ground. Then both planes were past and safe, although Wilk thought a few parting shots were sent their way.

Chappy leaned forward and handed him his notebook. *What happened?* was penciled in it. Wilk scribbled *Hand-grenade*, and passed it back. Chappy nodded, satisfied. Shao dropped toward Liangchow when they reached it and Wilk followed. It was wise to stop. They should check for damage.

But first things first. He practically leaped from his cockpit when the Avro came to a halt, and hurried to where Shao was lounging by his craft, looking far too self-satisfied. That made Wilk all the angrier. "That was incredibly foolish," he berated the pilot. "You jeopardized our mission for no reason."

Shao seemed astounded by this reaction. "If I can not trust you I shall turn around and return to Russia," Wilk warned. Not that he had any real intention of doing so.

The crestfallen captain seemed to have no response. Wilk softened. "Have you ever flown in actual combat, Captain Shao?" he asked.

"Ah — no. Not truly."

"I fought for four years. I know when one should attack and when one should run, and if there is nothing to be gained, one should always run."

"But I couldn't let them get away with that!" Shao attempted a lopsided smile.

"You could and you should. That is the discipline of a soldier. Let's see if your plane is damaged." He stopped short. "No, first, if you are damaged."

Shao was not damaged and, somewhat miraculously, neither was his Avro though there were a couple bullet holes in the wings. "Those should hold. I'll see about patching them up when we reach Lanchow," he said. "Ready to go again?"

Not one bullet had struck the machine Wilk flew. The sun was sinking into the mountains behind them when they saw the river and the Great Wall running on either side of it, glowing golden in the light. They had already passed over two spurs of that wall since leaving Liangchow. Beyond the river, the fabled Hwang Ho, the Yellow River, lay Lanchow.

There was a good field. The horses in it scattered as they landed.

26.

"I know about throwing grenades from airplanes," Wilk told the Chinese pilot. "Ground attack was my primary occupation in the last year of the war. Not that I didn't engage in it before then."

"This is why we need you at the school. You must teach us these things, the methods, the tactics."

"If I teach your would-be pilots how to get into the air and back to the ground without breaking their necks, I'll consider myself a success." If Wilk did stay and teach. He remained uncertain about it. "This is certainly an improvement in lodging."

They were ensconced in what was nearly a palace. Or perhaps it *was* a palace. They were the best rooms Wilk had seen since Tashkent. They would have been superior to Tashkent were they in better repair.

"We're not likely to find more comfort anytime soon," responded Shao. He sat silently for a moment before saying, "I must apologize for my recklessness today."

"And I apologize for losing my temper."

"You sounded like my old sergeant," said Chappy. "'E'd chew a man out proper, 'e would."

"Which you undoubtedly deserved. Do we press on tomorrow, Shao, or rest a day? If we've the time, the airplanes could use an hour or two of maintenance."

"I am not sure, Wilk. Someone knew we would fly through the pass and was ready for us. I do not feel safe lingering."

"The question is whether they know where we're 'eadin' next," Chappy pointed out.

Wilk nodded. "That is true and it gives me an idea. We tell everyone we fly south to Chungking and start out in that direction."

Chappy laughed. "And then turn the other way? Good idea!"

"So we shall, Jean Wilk. Have you, ah, a rank that goes before that name?"

"Not now. And definitely not before the name Jean Wilk. I was

Oberleutnant Hans Patrokowski in the German service, though my name is actually Jan." He wondered how many times more he would explain that. As long as he was in China, no doubt. "I was assured if the war had continued another week or two I would have been promoted to Heptman Patrokowski and given a command to go with it."

"Heptman?"

"The equivalent of captain. But I belong to no army now and have no wish to bear any rank." He looked straight at the young aviator. "And will not accept one if I teach at your flight school."

"'Ere, 'ere," said Chappy.

"That is not for me to say," was Shao's only response. "But I will say we should remain here tomorrow and rest and fix anything that may be wrong with the Avros. Then, um, south to Chungking!"

"Sounds good," said the Englishman. He hesitated a moment before asking, "Do y' expect we'll get shot at again?"

"I would count on it," Wilk told him.

Chappy shook his head. "Twice is enough for me. And 'ere we are without a rifle t' shoot back."

"A machine gun would be better," felt Shao.

"But more weight than we want to carry, even if we could mount one."

"The lighter we are the quicker we c'n run!" Chappy seemed pleased with that idea.

"True enough," Wilk said. "And the higher we can climb the safer we are from both guns and mountain tops."

So a day later they set out, fully fueled and carrying extra cans of petrol. How soon they might find more was uncertain. Shao was uncertain, anyway. Wilk suspected he would still have preferred to head for Chungking.

They did turn that direction. In fact, they would have turned that way whichever route they chose, for they followed the course of the main road south and a little east for some time. It was yet morning when they reached a river and a splitting of the road; one way went south into Szechwan, one followed the tumbling stream toward Sian. They had worked this out before leaving Lanchow. There was no need to land before turning east.

It was a country of wild valleys and gorges, the rounded mountains of many a Chinese painting. And it fell before them, into an ever-wider river valley. This river — what was it named? — would join the Hwang Ho further down but they would leave it at Sian. Wilk was relieved to see that town appear before the sun disappeared behind the mountains they had crossed.

There was the railroad terminus. He wondered if their former companions on the road, those two uncouth Chinese drivers, had reached it. Maybe they had flown over them at some time in the last few days, or even today. There had been a fair amount of traffic on the winding roadway below.

Shao descended toward a likely field near the river and what was certainly the army camp. A number of unfriendly-looking soldiers, rifles held ready, ran to surround them. "Here's the test," the captain called across to Chappy and Wilk. "Whether they like Sun enough to like us!" He stood in his cockpit, holding his papers aloft in one hand and proclaiming he had orders from the highest authorities to be here.

At least it was enough to keep them from being shot right then. A sergeant gave the papers a quick glance — there was no telling whether he could actually read them — and ordered all three to follow him to his superiors.

"This region is nominally under the control of the government," Shao confided to his companions. "Barely. Warlords hold power in much of China, you know. Local governors, generals, even bandit chieftains, have set themselves up as rulers in their own areas. Most here in the south give official recognition to the government in Canton but many ignore it otherwise." He looked around. "I'm not really sure of the current situation here in Sian."

A crowd had gathered to gape at the airplanes. Shao attempted to

117

impress on the sergeant the need to post guards. Two men were sent back with orders to keep watch. The rest escorted the newly-arrived trio to the nearest officer.

This man, apparently a full major, looked over their orders and then looked over the men. It probably did not take long for him to decide there were no bribes to be taken here. "I see no reason you can not stay the night here, the general approving. As for petrol —" He shook his head. "That is scarce and needed." And not for beggars who dropped from the sky.

The general apparently did approve, after they cooled their heels in the major's office for the better part of an hour. "We offer you our humble hospitality for the night," said the officer, in tones that suggested they should not refuse. "Corporal, show them to their room."

"I shall need to give the airplanes a good checking over before we depart," Wilk told him. "Tonight or early in the morning."

The man nodded with obvious disinterest. "As you wish. But I ask you to remain in the barracks overnight, for your own safety."

Perhaps it was for their safety. Or perhaps someone suspected them of being spies. It didn't matter. The room was adequate. Probably officers' housing. There were two cots. Wilk felt it best to make no mention of this and sleep on the floor. "Pretty country, 'ere," Chappy remarked. "Wouldn't mind so much if we 'ave to stay a little while."

Wilk had no intention of staying a little while. "We may have enough fuel left to get us down to Wuchang," he said, "but I'd rather not test it."

Shao agreed. "It is a long flight. It might test us too."

"No place to put down?" Chappy asked.

"Possibly. But that also I would rather not test."

"Mmm. Ready t' go check over the planes?"

"Too dark," felt Wilk. "We'd best wait for morning."

"I think we *do* need t' give 'em a look," insisted Chappy. Wilk recognized the Englishman had some sort of scheme. Shao remained oblivious, but followed them out into the dusk.

Two soldiers remained to guard the Avros. Most of the curious had moved on. "First we need t' get the petrol out of those cans and into the fuel tanks," Chappy said. Loud and matter-of-fact he spoke, but in English so the Chinese soldiers had no idea what he was saying. "Then we take the cans and refill them at the garage over there." He nodded in the direction of the building.

"Without asking?" wondered Shao.

"We did ask," Wilk pointed out.

Shao was willing to recognize the logic of that. In fact, once the fuel tanks were full, he ordered one of the soldiers to take a couple cans and follow him. "You'll have to stay and keep an eye on the planes, Wilk," he said. "Come on, Chappy."

A few minutes later, they reappeared with four filled cans. Moreover, they carried them in a borrowed automobile. "If we're official enough to requisition petrol, we're official enough to requisition transportation," Shao said. "Or so Chappy advised me. I wouldn't have thought of it."

"We'll hang these in the morning when I check over the engines," decided Wilk. "We've been running these engines on less than optimal fuel for some time. That's one reason I worry about them. Hmm, too bad you didn't grab some oil while you were at it."

"It's not too late," asserted Chappy.

"Let's not tempt fate. Best return the car and get to our quarters. And —" He turned to the two soldiers and thanked them for their vigilance and aid. Then he slipped each a couple coins. "Let's go."

"You have learned the way to do things here," spoke Shao as they motored back to the garage.

"It's the way everywhere in the world," Chappy assured him.

27.

It was not at all surprising that no one in authority knew of their appropriation of 'scarce and needed' petrol. The Avros launched into the sky as soon after dawn as practical. The trio of travelers had been offered no breakfast.

From Sian they must cut across the highlands to find the valley of the Han Kiang and follow the river down to Wuchang, where it joined the Yangtze. It was possible to do it in one day of steady flying. That would drain a man but not drain their fuel tanks — not with the extra ones Wilk had installed back at the start of their journey. They shouldn't have to tap the extra cans they had filled in the night. Those hung on either side of both airplanes.

They needn't set down at Wuchang itself. There were a number of large towns around Tungting Lake. Any would probably do. Then the last stage, the flight to Canton. Two days, if all went right. Never, if all went wrong!

It was no more than late morning when they spied the river and a decent sized town beside it. The map had told them if they hit the Han Kiang far enough north they would find the place. Shao gestured that he intended to land. An hour or so on the ground would do them all good, men and machines.

"Yunyang, I am fairly certain," announced Shao when they descended from their planes. They had landed in what was probably a major roadway. It would be hard to avoid the curious. "Are there soldiers here?" he called to a group of youngsters.

No. All called off to some other place. Would he like to talk to the policeman? They could run and fetch him!

"Let him come if he wishes," Shao told them. "The mayor too, and his wife!" Most laughed at his joke. One or two might not have known it was a joke and looked ready to go find the mayor.

"Are you going to check over your engines?" he asked Wilk.

"*My* engines? I don't own them, Captain. I am but their devoted servant, tending their needs. Anyway, they are too hot right now."

"Then let us tend to the needs of our stomachs. Ho, you!" He gestured toward the largest boy and held up a coin. "Yours if you keep an eye on the airplanes. Do not allow any of these dangerous ruffians too close!" It was not far to a street of booths, some selling food. Yunyang was a good-sized town, after all, not a mountain village. They filled themselves on noodles before returning to the planes, intact and scrupulously guarded by the lad Shao had left in charge. Shao paid him more than promised. Wilk gave the engines only a perfunctory inspection. They had been running well through the morning.

"Should we top off the tanks?" asked Chappy.

"I wouldn't take the time."

They flew on. This was now the China Wilk had long anticipated, rice paddies spread on the hillsides below him. It was still green, despite the beginnings of fall weather. Green compared to the lands he had passed through getting here!

The river, flowing almost east at Yunyang, curved ever more to the south. Steep hills were giving way to rolling farmland. And it was growing late. Where was the city Shao had chosen as their destination? There was a glimmer on the horizon, south of them. Lakes, more than one of them. They would need to turn east to reach Wuchang.

Shao fell back, signaled that he intended to land, and lazily descended toward the ground, falling into the shadows of the dusk. He chose a landing spot and glided into it. Wilk followed. It appeared to be a recently harvested field. Would an irate farmer come out and evict them?

Or maybe they had not even been noticed. It was almost night.

Shao explained himself. "Better to camp here, rather than attempt to find Wuchang or any other town in the dark. Perhaps it is just as well to avoid the cities anyway."

"What about fuel?" asked Chappy.

"The petrol in the cans should be sufficient," felt Wilk. "Possibly we do not even need that."

121

Shao agreed. "If it's not enough, we can find more tomorrow. This is a populous country and we shall pass over more towns."

"We might as well fill the tanks right now." That accomplished, they settled down to a cold supper. Lights could be seen here and there. Villages? The lone houses of peasants? They didn't know and never would. They had come in the dark, unseen strangers.

And they left in the dark, taxiing across the empty field and launching themselves into a sky tinged low on the eastern horizon with the pale peach of impending dawn. Wilk thought he glimpsed a single startled face staring up at them and then it was gone. There was just enough gray light to keep Shao's Avro in sight ahead of him. He would have to trust Shao to keep his eye on his compass.

Below, the wide winding river, the Yangtze, mighty even this far up its stream and then a great lake, shimmering in the dawn. Tungting. He would much like to come back here and see it in the daylight some-time. Perhaps in the moonlight as well.

Then all was left behind. Towns he spied, to their right, along a river that bent away from them and was lost to sight. The country grew more rugged again beneath them though it could not be compared to the mountains they had crossed. There were farms here.

Perhaps three hours had passed, three uneventful hours of good progress, when the rotary engine began to cough and miss. He adjusted his throttle, pulled even with Shao, motioned his desire to descend. The Chinese pilot gave a quizzical look — as quizzical as possible through goggles — and nodded. Both searched for a good spot to land. There were fields, there were roads, none ideal but adequate if this turned into an emergency. Surely a larger town was somewhere ahead. Kanchow, maybe. Not the Kanchow they had passed through before but another of the same name. He remembered seeing it on the map. Too far east of their path, maybe.

Chappy leaned forward and patted him on the shoulder. He pointed to a field a mile or two to their right, to the west. It looked good and only a little off their route. He banked toward it, expecting Shao to follow. The engine sounded worse, sputtering as he straightened out again. Then it didn't sound at all.

Close enough to glide, close enough to glide. So he told himself. It did look like a good field. In fact, it looked like an actual landing field. Yes, there was an airplane resting at one end. The shapes of trees rose toward him. Willows? There was no avoiding them. Wilk fought to keep his overloaded craft above the tree tops, the nose up but not so much as to induce a deadly stall, as he brought it to the correct angle for a landing. The Avro's wheels might actually have brushed the highest leaves. Then he was clear of them. He touched down and rolled to a stop.

Interview, Part Ten

The flight to Poland waited at the terminal. "When were you last in the country of your birth?" I asked.

"Thirty-one? No, Thirty-two. Those would be official visits. I had broken with the government back in Twenty-seven. With Pilsudski. But I didn't become persona non grata in Poland until I declared myself a member of the opposition in the early Thirties."

I had to smile at that 'official.' "There were off-the-record visits, I take it?"

"To be sure. I had to say goodbye to my mother and friends in Thirty-five, before I left Europe again." He seemed to think of those long gone friends and relatives for a few seconds. "I was also unwelcome in post-war Poland, but I slipped in once, on a French passport. Now my old friend Karol has fixed things up."

"Karol?"

Rita smiled. "He means the Holy Father."

"I met him in Rome shortly after the war. There were a number of young Polish priests in the city. I never thought they'd amount to much."

"It is good you were wrong about that," said his wife.

"Yes. It is. I had changed my mind by the time I saw Karol again at the Council in Sixty-two. I heard of the work he had done in Poland, standing up to the Communists. Is the flight ready yet?"

"In a while. Impatient, my dear?"

"I'm old. I haven't that much time!" Wilkins turned his attention back to me. "My story started with Poles and Russians and it seems to end with them."

"But there was much between. If you were not in Poland, where did you spend those years? The ones when you were not in China."

"I lived and worked mostly in Germany and France in the Thirties. The first half of the Thirties. As much of my time as possible was spent in this city." He turned his head to Rita. "We must stop longer here in

Paris on our way back."

"As long as you wish."

A call came for boarding the flight to Warszawa.

28.

The soldier spoke to them in what sounded much like the Mandarin Chinese he had learned yet Wilk could not make out any of the meaning. Shao answered in the same language.

"Cantonese?" he guessed.

"It is. The dialect is spoken everywhere in this part of the country. My own native tongue."

The Chinese soldier did not seem unfriendly. He did not point his rifle at them, but sent another man running toward the nearby buildings. That wasn't another Enfield, was it? No, some design Wilk had not seen before.

"We have come down at Colonel Peng's compound," Shao continued. "Perhaps two-hundred kilometers north of Canton." He sounded a tad unsure of that. "What happened to you?"

"The engine failed. I'll look at it when it has cooled down." Their hosts permitting.

"Mine seemed to be running rough too. Ah, here comes the colonel himself."

It seemed a well-maintained field but the only airplane in evidence was the old Caudron sitting at the far end. Wilk had seen Caudrons used as trainers in Russia but had never encountered one in his years of combat.

Shao saluted the colonel. Peng gave a leisurely return. He was a tall man, taller than any of the group of soldiers that had gathered, and somewhere in his middle years. He too spoke Cantonese to Shao for a minute or so.

Then he gave the Avros a looking over and spoke in Mandarin. "For the new flying school. I had heard there would be one. Major Li commands, no?"

"Yes sir," replied Captain Shao. "He reports directly to the republican government. They wanted a school independent of any, ah, local interests."

"Meaning warlords?" The colonel sounded amused. "Such as myself, I suppose. And my neighbors. Well, come along to my head-quarters, humble though they are."

As they accompanied him toward a group of low, tile-roofed structures, Peng continued. "I have become one of those they call warlords despite myself. I must protect the people here and keep this area I administer safe for the republic. And so I have taken on civil authority I did not want."

The soldiers were some of the best-groomed Wilk had seen — though their uniforms appeared far from new — and seemed well-disciplined. There was no slouching, at least around the colonel. It was a notable contrast to some of the slovenly troops they had encountered elsewhere.

"We must wire Canton that you are here," said the colonel, and then stopped to give the trio a long look. "Unless I keep you. I have no pilot and only one very poor airplane. I do not even know if it will fly."

"I would be glad to look at it, sir," volunteered Wilk. "We need to look at our own aircraft and, honestly, I am not completely certain they will fly again." He thought a moment. "Or I might need to rebuild the engines. That could take time. And tools and parts."

Some tools and parts had accompanied them. Not nearly enough, he suspected. Spark plugs and wrenches and little more.

"I thank you for your offer, Mister Wilk. It is Mister, is it not?" The colonel did not wait for an answer. "Corporal!" A smartly-uniformed man came running from the doorway of a small low building they had approached. Wilk noted at once that telegraph wires ran to it. "Send a wire to Canton informing them of this arrival. Three men and two airplanes. That is enough for now." He smiled thinly. "They can guess at anything more. Now come into my house, gentlemen."

It was the tallest structure in the compound, but not by much. There seemed to be but one story but it was raised some from the ground and a covered veranda ran across the front. Perhaps there were cellars.

As all the buildings here, its stucco walls were painted white. No, whitewashed, it could be told as they came closer. They mounted four broad red-tiled stairs to the porch. A flag of the Republic of China hung between posts supporting the roof.

Shao whispered to his companions. "I understand the colonel's wife and daughter live with him. It would be customary in most Chinese homes to address them as 'Peng's wife' and 'Peng's daughter,' if one must directly address his family at all. Here, I am not so sure. Peng is rather modern and, moreover, a Christian."

The Christian part became evident as soon as they stepped inside. A crucifix hung on the wall to their right, and printed pictures of Jesus and Mary, above a small carved table bearing a single red candle. Catholic, thought Wilk. That intrigued him a little. What route led a Chinese military officer to Rome?

Peng fired off rapid Cantonese to a wizened middle-aged woman who hurried away. "Rooms will be prepared for you," he said. "You will of course stay in my home. Step into my library please." The colonel might call it a library but it was clearly his office as well, his center of operations here. A large map hung on one wall, with an area marked off in blue ink. A number of villages lay within it, with words penciled in beside some of them.

Shao gave it a look. "We are here," he told Wilk and Chappy, pointing toward a spot toward the south of the outlined area. "Somewhat to the east of Shiuchow and Nanan." His finger moved to those two towns.

They lay outside what was undoubtedly Peng's area of authority. "And our destination is Canton. There," said Wilk, pointing. Not so far.

The captain nodded. "The field lies eight kilometers or so north of the city. Northeast."

No more than two hours flight from here. An hour and an half, more likely.

"I'll send you on your way in time," Peng told them. "Canton can practice patience for a day or three."

"Longer if our engines are ruined," Wilk replied.

"What is wrong with them?"

Wilk gave his companions a sidelong look. "Bad fuel is my guess. Maybe the petrol we obtained in Sian. Ordinary automotive fuel is bad enough in these finicky Gnomes but this was seemingly something worse."

"Fuel we have. Oil too. Castor oil — that is what you want, isn't it? Produced right here in China."

"We could certainly use it." The woman reappeared and murmured a few words.

"Ah, your rooms are prepared." He addressed her briefly. "Baths too. Please follow Martha."

A bath! There had not been the opportunity to soak in one since Ansi. They could worry about their gear in the planes later. Wilk suspected everything would be quite safe in Peng's compound.

And to Chappy's delight, their clothes disappeared while they bathed and robes of silk were provided.

29.

"I answer directly to the command in Canton," Colonel Peng informed them. "Not to any of the warlords in this region. Never the less, I must deal with them. Now, let us forget such things and eat."

With that he said a blessing in a language Wilk thought familiar but could not quite place, and they began their meal. It was a simple meal, despite the fine china and the broad carved table on which it was served. They exchanged a few words of no import but mostly concentrated on getting a good meal into themselves. Peng's wife, a quiet woman whose round face seemed to wear a constant smile, took a place at the other end of the table. There was no sign of the rumored daughter.

Peng looked down the length of the table at her, after a while. "Luisa is being left out, I fear. She does not follow Mandarin very well and English not at all. Do you gentlemen speak French?"

Chappy and Shao had to admit their ignorance. Wilk admitted his fluency. "The three of us can plot secretly now against my companions, Madame Peng," he told the woman.

Mrs. Peng giggled politely and remained quiet no longer. Indeed, she became quite voluble, chatting on in French through the meal. She spoke of their eighteen year old daughter, Mary, who was in school in Macao. Oh, and her husband had gone to school there too. His family lived near the city and had been Catholic for generations and all spoke Portuguese. Mary hoped to go to Europe to study medicine next year. She might learn something of nursing in Victoria first. The sunflowers had bloomed very beautifully this year. Luisa came from a Catholic family too, down in the French enclave, and many of them did business in Tonkin and Annam.

Wilk listened to this with one ear as Peng switched languages back and forth but rarely said anything more than a few words.

"Is there a Catholic priest near?" Wilk asked. "Or Christian ministers of any sort?"

The colonel scowled at that. "Only missionaries who do more harm than good, unless one goes to the larger towns. A priest visits here from time to time."

"His church is in Kanchow," added his wife.

"We are the only Catholics here so he really shouldn't bother with us. Of course, there is a cathedral in Canton and we can be driven to Macao in a day's time," said Peng. "Too many priests there! Ah, the brandy." A young soldier brought a tray with decanter and glasses. "That is one of the things the missionaries preach against. Some of them."

"All things in moderation is my religion," stated Chappy, pouring himself a short brandy. "I 'ear some Greek said that ages ago."

"And it is just as good advice today," said Wilk, lifting his glass. "To moderation."

Shao shrugged and perhaps smiled to himself before raising his own glass. The captain was not one to value compromise; Wilk had already seen that in him. He envied it some, the ability to be sure about things, to follow a cause without question. He could never do that.

He realized of a sudden that Peng was addressing him. "You are both a pilot and a mechanic, Monsieur Wilk?"

"So it would seem, sir. I was first the one and then the other in the German air service. Now, I must take on both occupations." He almost left it there but added, "When I return home, I may finish my degree as an engineer." If he returned home.

"A most useful calling though we need your other skills at this time. You studied in Poland? There are good schools?"

"I studied in Berlin. That is not so far from my home, a day or so by rail." Wilk paused, realizing something he had not thought of before. "But it is no longer in the same country."

"Ah, yes, Poland is independent now. Perhaps they will have good schools of their own." Almost as an afterthought, he said, "We need more good schools in China."

"Our daughter will study in Paris," said Luisa. "Have you been to

Paris, Jean?"

"No, Madame, though the German army did its best to get me there."

Peng chuckled at the quip. "But you must visit the city someday. And Rome. Luisa and I made a pilgrimage there when we were first married."

"Our honeymoon," said Madame Peng, smiling.

"I shall attempt to see them both," Wilk promised.

"And I would enjoy seeing more of your compound here, sir," said Shao. "But after we have a good night's sleep, perhaps."

"We should unload our gear," Chappy put in.

"It will be safe," said Colonel Peng. "Unless you need something immediately?"

"It can wait," Wilk decided. He expected no contradiction from the others.

Each man had been given a small room of his own but all three gathered in Wilk's, crowding into the space. The house was not new; that they could see. It had undoubtedly been built for some local man of importance, the summer home, perhaps, of a landowner of some sort or even a bureaucrat of the old imperial regime.

Wilk and Chappy sat on straw mats on the dark wooden floor. Shao perched on the end of the low bed. "What do you think of this Peng?" he asked.

"I'm inclined to trust 'im more than just about anyone we've met since leavin' Russia," said Chappy. "'E's a gentleman."

"I mistrust him. He is half a foreigner, with his ties to the Portuguese and the French." A slight smile, perhaps of embarrassment, crossed the captain's face. "Not that I have anything against foreigners, mind you, but China must be put first."

Wilk had heard Poles say quite similar things. It might be best not to bring that up. "People will take up new ways," he said. "That is inevitable."

"Well do I know it. I was born and grew up in Hong Kong — the

city the British name Victoria. Many have taken up new ways there."
He laughed and rose. "The republic itself is a new way. I certainly have
no desire to return to imperial rule. So instead I shall go to my bed."
With a slight bow, Shao slipped out.

"'Ong Kong," mused Chappy. "That's just down the river from
where we're 'eaded, isn't it? Maybe I should aim t' get there. After a
while, y' know?"

"I thought you wanted to avoid British territory," said Wilk.

"I could use another name. Like you. Mmm." The Englishman
considered for a moment. "From now on Thomas Chapman is dead.
I'm Charles Thomas. Call me Charlie."

"I'm too used to calling you Chappy."

"I reckon it won't 'urt any if you do. 'Specially seein' as Thomas
Chapman got 'imself killed back in Russia."

"And so I shall report," Wilk promised him. Chappy went to his own
room. Wilk assumed his companions slept as well as he.

30.

"That's a French airplane, right?" asked Chappy.

"It is," agreed Wilk.

Chappy gave it a long looking over. "The French are an odd bunch," he finally stated.

The Caudron was a rather preposterous looking craft. It had the open-work twin booms of a typical pusher but the engine in the central nacelle was instead in the tractor position, making the booms a somewhat pointless exercise in increased drag. That engine he could see was a rotary, possibly a le Rhone. Probably lower power than the Gnomes fitted to the Avros.

Lateral control was by wing-warping, not ailerons. The Caudron was a thoroughly antiquated machine, even for training. It sat across the field from their own airplanes. Wilk would look at them later. At the moment, a trio of soldiers was removing their gear under Shao's direction.

It was a pleasant field in a pleasant setting. Better suited to a flock of sheep, he felt, than airplanes. A lake lay close by, behind a screen of hanging willow branches. He could hear ducks. It was good fortune it had lain in their path. The last time Wilk had an engine fail on him he had ended up with a smashed airplane and broken ribs.

He and Chappy joined Captain Shao, leading his minions toward the house. Luisa Peng came down from the porch to greet them. Two fat pugs followed at her heels, one black, one tawny. Her costume was completely Western this morning. Wilk could imagine his own mother in that white, high-collared blouse and long dark skirt.

"Come join us for breakfast, Gentlemen," she called, in French. Shao and Chappy would have to adapt to that; Madame Peng had apparently decided to communicate with her guests solely in that tongue.

The colonel was already at the head of the table. As soon as they were seated — their belongings being sent along to their rooms — he again asked a blessing. Wilk recognized the language now as Portuguese.

A dark young man ate with them. His uniform proclaimed him a lieutenant. He and the colonel carried on a conversation in Cantonese, a conversation Wilk could not follow. Shao surely could but politely appeared to take no notice.

Peng's adjutant, perhaps, discussing the day's agenda with him. Wilk turned his own attention to the breakfast. There were many eggs, boiled or maybe steamed. Chicken or duck? He supposed it didn't matter much. Rolls. Rice. Cheese? He took a slice, clumsily with his chop-sticks, and attempted an unobtrusive sniff. It didn't smell like cheese.

"Bean curd," whispered an amused Shao. "You may like it."

Only one way to find out. Yes, it was decent. Bland. Wilk did not mind bland. But he would have to practice the use of the sticks.

The tea was good. He ate well but not heavily. "I should check our airplanes and their engines," he announced. "Yours as well, Colonel."

"I would be grateful for that, Monsieur Wilk," the officer replied. "You will have to send one of your students from Canton to fly it for me."

"I suspect I may spend more time teaching mechanics than pilots," said Wilk. He had not had time, nor much reason, to think about the school during their travels. Now he was almost there and it was becoming quite real.

"I am sure those are needed too. Ye here will provide anything you need, or translate for you."

The young officer gave them a sober nod.

Wilk took his time walking out to the waiting Avros, and then walked around them, looking for any glaring structural problems. None. He hadn't expected any but it was best to check this first. The wire bracing, in particular. All seemed well enough though it could be tightened up here and there. That would have to be by eye and by feel, as before. There was no official manual, no calipers nor gauges, to work from.

Good enough. The engines — "Can you find me some alcohol, Lieutenant Ye? The more pure, the better."

"Alcohol?" asked Chappy. "You think there might be water in the fuel?"

"Possibly. Among other things. Why don't you see about draining the tanks?" He then busied himself with partially dismantling and cleaning the engines. They were not as bad as he feared. He might not even need to replace any parts. Not now. After the two hour flight to Canton, it might be a good idea — assuming parts were available there.

"I would like to lay some of these parts out to check over and clean before reinstalling them," he told Ye. "Is there a workshop?"

There was. The lieutenant directed his men to carry away the pieces Wilk pointed out. It was only past mid-morning. "I believe I shall check over the Caudron," announced Wilk.

He would have no problem with its engine. He knew it better than the Gnome, in fact, having worked on both French le Rhones and German copies of the design. First, a quick looking over of the machine, as he had with the Avros. It looked tight. Then, into the cockpit, checking all the controls. Everything moved when it should, the elevators, the rudder. The wing-warping system seemed to function. Wilk climbed back down. "Put some air in those tires," he directed. "And check ours too."

Then the rotary engine. He shook his head. "What is wrong, sir?" asked Ye. He spoke rather good French, though with an obvious accent.

"Filthy. It's going to need a good cleaning. Hmm, might not hurt to put some alcohol in its tank too, if you have it. And I'll need oil."

Wilk decided to put all his effort into the Caudron for the rest of the morning. If pressed, he might have been willing to admit that he liked working on something different. He'd grown weary of nursing the Avros and their Gnomes.

The sun stood overhead when he climbed again into the cockpit. "Want to ride along?" he called to Ye. The young officer gave an emphatic shake of his head. "You might let the colonel know I'm going to test it." Ye immediately sent a man running with this news.

"Chappy, do ground crew duties, will you? The prop and the chocks."

It took more than one spin of the propeller for the engine to catch but it eventually did. Smooth enough, felt Wilk. He could see Colonel Peng approaching, four men clutching rifles following behind. Wilk waved to him and yelled for Chappy to pull away the wheel chocks. These were attached to a single rope.

Then he was taxiing across the field. Wilk did not attempt to take off. He wanted the feel of the aircraft on the ground first. Where was the wind? The flags fitfully stirred in a light breeze. Probably not enough to matter one way or another but he could put his nose toward it. The Caudron came around and he opened the throttle. It lumbered down the field and into a takeoff.

Not so bad, thought Wilk. Nothing like the responsiveness of the Avro but it handled well enough. He did a circuit of the field, rising no higher than the tree tops and brought the aircraft back into a landing.

As he hopped to the ground, Peng told him, "I was not altogether certain you would return to us. I am glad I was right in trusting you."

"I am glad your men did not point their rifles at me. What are they? I'm not familiar with the design."

The officer had to laugh at the sudden shift in their conversation. "Those are the new Springfield rifles the Americans have supplied. Maybe not new, precisely, but new to us. There are said to be Marlin machine guns too but those we have not seen."

"The Colt pistols, too, sir," Shao added. "Such as I carry."

"A fine weapon," admitted the colonel. "I prefer my Mauser. The 'box cannon' my men call it."

"It seems, ah, unwieldy," ventured Wilk. The Mauser was large for a pistol. It looked almost like a small rifle. That resemblance would increase if Peng attached its shoulder stock, which doubled as an holster.

"Perhaps so. It is the most powerful pistol available. More than your Colt, Captain, though its bullet is not quite so heavy."

"And mine is lighter and less powerful than either," said Wilk.

"Ah, the French service revolver. I have seen many of them but mostly on Frenchmen."

"French or not, I am growing rather fond of this revolver. I may just stick with it. But now," Wilk continued, "I should stick with the task of getting the Avros back into the air."

Interview, Part Eleven

"You know I became even more fond of the Browning Hi-Power pistol later. I was carrying it when you first met me in Vietnam."

"Yes, I remember it well and I remember you said you had carried it since the Thirties."

"Since Thirty-six to be exact. Raoul Guzman presented me with one then. The president of El Plantio. We were old friends."

I knew that story pretty well. I knew also that Rita was born in El Plantio. "But you carried the French revolver before that?"

"Yes, the *Modele 1892*, called erroneously the Lebel by some. I carried the official Nagant revolver when I served Poland, but the 1892 remained my preference. It never let me down."

"Yet you switched eventually."

"I did. I may speak of it like an old friend but I am not sentimental when it comes to my tools. The Browning is simply a better pistol. It fires not only a more powerful round but it holds more of them. In my opinion, it remains the best pistol ever designed."

"So you have frequently claimed," chimed in Rita.

"And no one has disproved it to me."

31.

The Avros also flew before sundown, to the relief of both Wilk and Shao, though their reasons might have been different. Be that as it may, there would be no reason not to depart in the morning.

Both most certainly wanted to be on the way to Canton. Chappy, perhaps not so much. "I could stand another day or two of this place," he avowed. "And this warm weather."

"Canton rarely grows cold," Shao assured him. "It is actually in the tropics, though just barely. We shall fly across the tropic tomorrow."

"I wouldn't mind spendin' some time in a tropical paradise. Always thought I'd like that, y' know?"

"You might not think so when summer heat comes. You have missed that."

And I might miss it when it comes again, Wilk told himself. They dined as before with the Pengs. "Now that you have my air force in working order," said the colonel as the brandy was served, "I have even more incentive to keep you here."

Wilk was certain — almost certain — Peng jested. "I promise to return and help you with the airplane. It is not a long trip."

The officer gave this an amiable nod. "True. Even by automobile, no more than half a day."

"And," Wilk added, "I have not accepted any position at the flight school. My only pledge was to deliver the airplanes."

"Oh?" Peng glanced at Shao. "Your chaperon, I think, does not completely approve of your attitude. That reminds me, Shao, the latest 'Harbor' arrived this afternoon. That is the paper for which your father works, is it not?"

"It is, sir." He turned to his companions. "*The Harbor* is an English-language paper of Hong Kong, but published for a Chinese readership. My father is an editor and part-owner."

"My daughter reads it. That is why I have it sent here with the mail. Twice a week."

"There is not enough interest to print more frequently. Perhaps not enough interest to print as frequently as they do." There had been the slightest trace of sarcasm in his tone. He continued, more evenly. "The readers are few, mostly in Hong Kong, but a few copies are sold else-where. Canton, even Macao. As my father puts it, the readership is wide but not deep."

Peng smiled at this. "I would hazard you do not share the paper's internationalist views."

"Nor my father's. He espouses free trade and the breaking down of all barriers." Shao paused but a moment before saying, "I am a British subject but I chose to fight for the republic. The English will go someday. China will remain."

"I too support the republic. Yet we increasingly become one world. The airplane, the cables across the oceans. And now the wireless." Peng seemed to ponder the wonders of the modern world for a second or two. Or perhaps he pondered Shao. "But you are no traditionalist."

"I am not, sir. I believe it is better to shape what will come than attempt to prevent it."

"On this we can agree. Possibly Jean does not share that viewpoint, however?"

"I am content just to survive the present," stated Wilk. "And to do what I believe is right." That is the truth, isn't it? he asked himself. Jean Wilk — or Jan Patrokowski — had no strong political convictions. Certainly no nationalistic ones either.

"And let folks live their lives," Chappy said.

Wilk nodded his agreement. "Exactly."

"Yet you were sent here by communists," said Peng. "You do not have socialist leanings?"

"I'll leave those to Chappy."

"Can't say I'm that fond of 'em m'self anymore," said the Englishman. "Seen too much of 'em in Russia. Wilk 'ere is an anarchist at 'eart, I think."

"Ah, I can see this," laughed Captain Shao. "And as any true anar-

141

chist, a strong believer in self-control and individual responsibility."

This talk made Wilk at least a little uncomfortable. He had no desire to explore such things at the moment. Better to just get onto whatever was next.

"You are not a socialist, are you, Captain?" asked Peng.

"No. I may not agree with my father on some things but I have not moved that far from him. Free enterprise will build the new China — but it must be guided by the state."

Peng slowly nodded. "Very well," he said, "but who then will guide the state?"

"All of the wrong people," spoke Chappy. "As usual."

Wilk raised his glass and drank to that.

32.

The airfield lay seven or eight kilometers northeast of Canton. They could spy the city sprawling beyond it and a network of waterways around and beyond the city.

Departure from Peng's headquarters had been leisurely. They had enjoyed a breakfast and the companionship of the colonel and his wife before setting forth. No more than an hour and an half later, they were circling the air school.

A couple of good sized hangars, constructed of corrugated metal, stood on one side of the wide field. Huts and barracks were packed around the remainder of its perimeter, and several aircraft sat on the grass. There were some Caudrons, like the one back at Colonel Peng's field. Avros similar to their own. That was some sort of French bomber over there, Wilk was sure, a Breguet or a Salmson. He would have to see it closer up.

Then he followed Shao to a landing, and taxied into a spot beside the other Avro. The captain jumped down to greet a young officer headed their way. Unlikely to be a pilot, thought Wilk as he climbed down himself, more slowly. Not with the thick glasses he was wearing.

"Major Li can not greet us," Shao reported. "Lieutenant Cao will see to getting us squared away. He runs this base, in truth."

The young man only grinned and bobbed his head at them.

"This is Jean Wilk," Shao informed him, "and this is Charles Thomas. He is Wilk's driver and aide."

The man scanned the sheets of paper clipped to his board. "Wilk — yes." He nodded and lifted his eyes to peer at Chappy. "He is not listed. There is a T. Chapman." He looked about as if he expected the missing man to suddenly materialize.

"Killed back in Russia," Wilk told him. "Charlie was sent as his replacement. You were not informed?" He attempted to sound as incredulous as possible.

Cao stared at his papers again before shrugging. "Very well. C.

Thomas." He crossed out T. Chapman and wrote in the new name. "Have you a rank, sir?"

"You could call me Captain Wilk, if you wish, but I am a civilian now and have no intention of either saluting or being saluted."

"Monsieur Wilk, then." It had apparently been assumed he was French. His revolver might have added to the impression. The lieutenant's eyes again went to Chappy. "Will your aide share your quarters?"

"He might as well. And we must settle the question of our pay at once. Both of us. You know," he said, lowering his voice and leaning in as if imparting a confidence, "we traveled all the way across Asia without being paid."

Never mind that he still carried some of the traveling money they had been given, a portion of it in gold. That had been advanced to Orkovsky so his statement was technically true.

"I shall take care of it personally, sir," spoke Cao. Wilk suspected the lieutenant took care of all such things. He probably had papers ready for them to sign, formally handing over the Avros.

"Let's unload these airplanes and be done with them, Charlie," he said.

"I'll get some men to help with that," said Shao. "Lieutenant, can you put them into the quarters next to mine?"

Cao stared into space a moment, perhaps visualizing that arrangement. "Um, yes. Yes, I can, sir. I'll see to it." He glanced at his paperwork again. "And leave them to your care." With a salute, he turned and hurried off across the field.

"Can we expect other officers to speak Mandarin?" asked Wilk, watching Cao disappear.

"Yes, to be sure. The soldiers, not for the most part." The captain drafted a pair of those soldiers to assist them. "There should be a complete inventory," he decided. "Anything that is not personal should be listed before it is turned over. Signed by both of us."

Chappy was left out of that end of things and seemed grateful for it.

He would be not eager to have his signature — however he spelled it — on any documents. Most of the airplane-related equipment was turned over to the chief mechanic, a burly non-com who unfortunately spoke only Cantonese. Wilk saw that could be a problem. Then they embarked for their rooms.

"Rather Spartan," commented Wilk, on inspecting theirs. "Except we're in China, not Greece." It was small, with two iron-framed bunks below a cracked window.

"I advise spending as little time here as possible," said Shao.

"Where should we go? Into Canton?"

"If you desire. As soon as I am able, I will go down to Hong Kong and see my family."

"Your parents?"

"And my wife."

"Oh. If I had a wife, I wouldn't stay here either." Wilk's thoughts could not help be pulled to Axana. Why was he not with the little Turkoman girl? It was too late to follow her back across most of Asia but he could go down to the coast right now and take a ship.

Shao broke into his reverie. "Let's get to the mess. It's been long since breakfast." Very well. He would think about leaving later. Best to see how things stood here first.

"Y' know," Chappy whispered to him as they followed Shao, "it's just a year since the war ended."

"It seems like more," Wilk admitted.

"It certainly does."

33.

"The Republican Air Arm is disorganized and controlled by local factions. There are plans for an Aviation Ministry and true air force. This school," said Major Li, "is part of the preparation for that."

Wilk and Chappy had donned their Austrian uniforms, thoroughly cleaned at Peng's. They looked reasonably presentable. Shao was as impeccably accoutered as ever.

"You are certain you will not accept a commission?" the commandant again asked. "Our other foreign instructor has taken the rank of captain, and the pay that goes with it."

Meaning Wilk would not receive as much if he declined to join. That did not matter and he should be honest in telling this officer why. "I do not know if I will remain past this winter, sir. If that is not acceptable, I'll leave at once."

"It matters little. We shall list you as an adviser." Li's eyes flicked to Cao, seated to one side. The aide would take care of such things.

Major Li was a small wiry man with a trim mustache. "He looks like you 'cept Chinese," Chappy had whispered when they entered his office. Shao had told them the officer was a flier himself, not just an administrator posted here. One of the earliest pilots in the country, in fact, a disciple of Feng Ru, the nation's first aviator.

"And you —" The major's attention turned to Chappy. "We have no need for you here, not as a driver. And though our officers are assigned a personal aide, Monsieur Wilk is not to be an officer, it seems. So what shall we do with you?"

Before the Englishman could find an answer, Wilk spoke. "He will be my aide, none the less. If necessary, I shall pay his salary from my own wages."

Li smiled at this. "And you may move along in the spring too, Mister Thomas?"

"I expect so, sir. I'm no use to anyone 'ere but Captain Wilk."

Captain Wilk? Chappy had never referred to him so before. Still, it made sense he would now. Especially in that he seemed to be attaching himself to Wilk.

"See to it he is listed in some capacity," Li told his aide. Cao nodded. He would come up with something. The major turned back to Wilk. "Shao tells me you are an excellent mechanic but no more than an adequate pilot." He did not appear to take this assessment overly seriously. "Adequate is quite good enough but it is your experience in combat that will be most useful to our students. Ah, Captain Singleton. Come in."

A squat, broad-shouldered man in uniform stood in the open doorway. Wilk rose from his chair to greet him. "Captain Edward Singleton, I present Captain Jean Wilk." The two shook hands. The newcomer ignored Chappy and Chappy reciprocated.

"A Frenchy?" asked Singleton.

"German, according to his papers," said Li. "But not actually, I believe?"

"Polish, but I served with the Germans during the war." Again, it was necessary to explain this. "It might be simplest if I was known as a Pole here." That had been the original thought of the Reds who sent him, officially distancing themselves. Things might well have changed since he set out in the spring.

"Ah. Perhaps we exchanged gunfire at some time."

"It is possible."

"Show Captain Wilk around, will you?" asked Major Li. "Or Monsieur Wilk, as he refuses a military commission."

The English pilot saluted and turned toward the doorway. Wilk only nodded to the commandant before following. There were most certainly good points to remaining a civilian.

He should see about obtaining civilian clothes. Hong Kong's tailors were renowned, were they not?

"Shao and I are the senior instructors here," Singleton was saying. "There are usually two or three young fellows on staff to help with the actual flight training. Say, do you speak English?"

WILK

"I do," answered Wilk, switching from Mandarin.

"Jolly good. It will be nice to have someone besides Shao to talk to. I do get sick of hearing this Chinese sing-song."

Wilk turned his head, meaning to give Chappy a wink. Where had the man gone?

"We have the one Salmson," said Singleton, pointing it out, "for training bomber crew at the moment. And for training mechanics." The Salmson had a variant — or relative might be more accurate — of the radial engine Wilk had come to know and dislike in the Russian Anatras and Lebeds.

"And the pair of Ansaldos over there. They're quite new." Those were unfamiliar to Wilk.

"The Russians were flying castoff aircraft from both sides when I left. The Avros we arrived in are such." He peered down the line of aircraft. "The Ansaldos are fighters?"

"Fitted out as bombers, in fact, but they are capable combat aircraft. If it ever proves necessary to defend this field we shall have to depend on them." He did not sound overly confident about that eventuality. "But their purpose is advanced training."

Aside from being armed single-seaters and of Italian manufacture, Wilk knew nothing of the machines. The engines would be new to him, as well. They might prove interesting.

"We start the lads out in the Caudrons," the Englishman went on. "G-Threes. Ever flown one?"

"I have, at Colonel Peng's compound."

"Peng, eh? Another one of these petty warlords, I understand. China is a fine mess, Wilk, a fine mess, and I don't see anyone sorting it out. Not anyone Chinese."

"You think the British should step in?" Wilk tried not to sound amused as he said this.

There was a slow and solemn shake of Singleton's head. "Our day is done out here. Now the Japs — there's a fine bunch. Things would get done if they ran the show."

Knowing no Japanese, Wilk made no comment and kept his doubts to himself. It was not any of his concern. Singleton seemed to have no interest in touring the mechanics' shed so the two parted company. "We'll work up a schedule for you," the man promised.

Chappy was in their quarters when Wilk returned. "I'm officially an adviser too, now. The lieutenant saw to it. I may even 'ave t' teach some."

"Teach?"

"Firearms training. Just the thing for a pacifist, isn't it?"

"I can't think of any better choice," said Wilk.

Interview, Part Twelve

"There came a formal alliance between Russia and the Nationalists in Twenty-three and Soviet advisers were sent. Notably, Mikhail Borodin. You might say I was a forerunner of his sort in my way."

"But the communists were mistrusted."

"Yes, the honeymoon was brief. Chiang threw them all out a few years later. That was when I was invited to go back — and it happened I was at loose ends, having just resigned my government post in Poland."

I didn't need to check my notes for the next question. "That was in Twenty-seven?"

"Yes. I became disenchanted with Poland when Pilsudski made himself a dictator in all but name. I've mentioned that already, I am sure. Many times!" We both chuckled at that. "Not that I had been particularly enchanted with the Polish regime before then. So I jumped at the offer to return to China."

"As a pilot or an engineer?"

"Some of each, plus a little information gathering. The leaders knew I had some experience in such matters."

His future occupation. "For Poland."

"Primarily. The Soviet advisers did do good work on helping to modernize China while they were there and Russia continued to give aid. Orkovsky was briefly with them. He was able to go by sea that time. We missed running into each other, of course." Wilkins's face grew grave. "Which was undoubtedly good for his career. I would not have wanted to be the cause of him being caught up in a purge."

34.

The telegraph operator at the camp was quite emphatic that he could deal only with official business. He was also quite apologetic.

"I am sorry about this, sir. The rules are strict. If you wish to write out a message I can have someone carry it to the nearest office." That there would be some sort of tip involved, Wilk didn't mind. He did mind not delivering his messages in person. He wanted to be certain of things.

"How far to this office?" he asked.

"Perhaps six kilometers. At the railroad terminal in the city."

Wilk meant to visit Canton anyway. This gave him a reason to do it now. Shao was the man to see about it.

"I have no doubt Russia has been officially informed that airplanes and pilot have arrived, but I would like to send a message to Lieutenant Orkovsky, if I could, telling him."

And one to his parents, as well. They should know he was alive!

"You don't know where the man is, do you?" asked the captain.

"Chances are he is yet to arrive in Tashkent. I could send a wire to the government offices there to await his arrival. The Reds might even appreciate a telegram from me assuring them of the mission's success. It wouldn't get Kolya in any trouble, anyway."

But getting a message to Kasim? More difficult. Ah, yes, he could ask after their guide, only telling Orkovsky where he could be reached and hoping he might pass that information on.

And he would write a letter to his family later, to follow the telegram. None of this would raise any problem except that of expense. A letter to Russia? Who could say whether that would ever reach its intended recipient? Hmm, Adrik, that would be the man. But what was the family name? Wilk realized he didn't know, had never heard it, seen it written.

That was, no doubt, intentional.

"We'll make a day of it tomorrow," promised Shao. As a senior instructor, he could arrange schedules as he wished. Within reason.

Wilk had undertaken his first turn as an instructor that afternoon, coaxing a pair of youngsters into making short hops along the field in one of the Caudrons. He had also, with the help of Lieutenant Cao, been able to communicate with the mechanics, doing no more than complimenting them and Sergeant Zhang on the condition of the aircraft. He would have to find a more readily available interpreter. Or learn to speak the Cantonese dialect.

Then he could point out their mistakes. Shao was ready with a staff car and driver first thing in the morning. "You might as well come along, Mister Thomas," he said. "Ride in the front."

Chappy climbed in beside the soldier at the wheel, while Shao and Wilk occupied the rear seat. It was a Ford, a Model T, such as Wilk had traveled with on the caravan road. He noted that Shao carried his Colt but that was normal when he was in uniform. He even wore it while instructing neophyte fliers.

Wilk had tucked his own revolver unobtrusively into a holster inside the waist band of his trousers. The air was cool enough to keep the concealing but constricting jacket buttoned up — but that would make it harder to reach the weapon in need.

What need would there be? He was past the dangers of their long journey.

Canton was a city of waterways, an inland port, and more than one canal was crossed as they drove directly to the rail station. "The railway here does not connect to the rest of China," said Shao. "Not yet. It only runs down to Hong Kong and a little way up the river."

This had no bearing on the wires Wilk wished to send. The telegraph office was easily located. A clerk looked over the first form he filled out, the message to his parents in Poland.

"What language is this, sir?"

"German."

"I must ask what it means, for the official record."

That was understandable. Messages in strange languages would be suspect. "Tear it up," he said. "I'll write in English instead."

English presented no problem. His father read the language and the telegraph office was used to it. *safe canton china stop will write soon* — that was enough, wasn't it? Hmm, maybe not. Wilk added, *love all*, to what he had already printed out. He could afford the extra words. The cost was steep but acceptable. Wilk wondered which way it would be routed. Through Asia? Across two oceans? No matter, as long as it arrived.

Then there was the telegram to Tashkent. He had no idea how to write out a message in Cyrillic Russian nor would the telegraph oper-ator know how to send it. Best he compose that in English as well. Compose it carefully.

"Anyone you want to send a telegram to, Chappy?" he asked when his task was completed. "Family in England?"

"Best they believe I'm dead, I reckon."

There was no good reply to that. "I should send a letter to my family next," said Wilk. "If I'd been thinking, I'd already have written it and have it with me."

"Better to mail it from Hong Kong," Shao told him, "and entrust it to the British postal service. Give it to me when you're ready and I'll post it the next time I go down."

"Very well. So what does one do with a free day in Canton?"

Shao smirked — or came close to it. "Visiting bars and brothels is popular."

"I dare say. I think I need to buy some new clothes."

"That y' do," agreed Chappy. "Me too. I'm sick of dressin' like a soldier."

"Then we shall find you a tailor." Shao threw rapid-fire instructions in Cantonese at the driver.

They drove toward the center of the city, through the crowded bustling streets. Wilk noted that ugly looks were occasionally turned their way. It was not surprising that some here would dislike foreigners. He looked upward and drew a deep breath in surprise.

WILK

Gulls! Ah, he should have expected there would be seabirds here, close to the coast. Here were the gulls of which he had told Axana, gulls as in that port on the other side of the world. His home. He watched them soar and tumble for a couple minutes, letting nothing else intrude on this pleasure, before turning his eyes again to the streets of Canton.

"Stop!" He shouted suddenly and jumped from the Ford as it rolled to a halt before the open doors of a garage.

"Are you thinking of buying a car?" Shao called after him. There were two outside at the curb with signs and probably more within.

Wilk shook his head and pointed to the sign. *Feng and Sons Automobiles for Sale and Hire*, it read in wobbly English letters, and beneath that, *Motorbikes*.

"A cycle could be just the thing for me," he said. "I messed about with motor bikes as a boy. Before the war."

"Every mechanic needs to start somewhere," observed Shao. "Let's take a look."

"It could get me around almost as quickly as a plane," Wilk, already inside the brick building, threw back to him over his shoulder.

By the time Shao and Chappy caught up, he was looking over three motorbikes lined up in the dim light admitted through a high window, streaked with filth. Two appeared to be bicycles with tiny motors attached in improbable positions. The third was a true motorcycle. "An Indian. That's an American bike, I know, but I've never seen one before."

A portly man approached, wiping his hands on a dirty rag. A thin greasy beard graced his chin. "No run," he declared, inclining his head toward the Indian. "No fix can." Wilk assumed the man spoke only an English pidgin and Cantonese.

Wilk shrugged and assumed a resigned look. "Too bad. No parts?"

The man only shook his head. "Bad engine," he declared, and no more. Wilk squatted and looked more closely. No cracks or obvious damage, but who could tell what was truly wrong without dismantling

154

it? It might be an enjoyable project. He had already become a little bored with the air school routine.

Wilk made what he was fairly sure was a ridiculous offer for the bike. He was surprised when the mechanic came back with one only slightly higher. "Done," he said, and shook the greasy hand. "Let's get this lashed to the back of the Ford."

As they were tying it in place, Chappy leaned in, whispering, "Don't look but I believe I've seen that man across the street followin' us earlier."

"Do we not all look the same to you?" asked Captain Shao. He did not seem to take Chappy's statement seriously.

"Maybe so, but I remember 'is clothes."

Wilk almost without thinking loosened the coat concealing his revolver. "Let's keep an eye open," he said, "and go see about our own clothes."

35.

Shirts. They purchased shirts of silk and of linen, and ties, and sturdy trousers for everyday wear. And two suits, also of silk, were ordered to be delivered in a couple days. Wilk's was of sober cut and color.

Chappy had declared, "If this is the tropics, I'm bloody well goin' t' dress like it," and ordered his in white.

"We can worry about boots some other time," Wilk decided. He was not inclined to spend all his money at once. Chappy, he feared, was. Still, the cost of it all had been pleasingly low.

It was late afternoon and the narrow streets were filling with shadow. Chappy turned around to speak to Wilk and Shao. "There's that fellow again," he said. "The one in the brown bowler."

"Keeping an eye on us for someone, you think?" wondered Wilk. The auto had slowed down as pedestrians crowded close on either side.

"Perhaps," allowed Shao. "There are factions. You are aware of that."

Only too aware. The man in the brown bowler had stepped up onto the edge of a fountain and was haranguing the crowd. The language was Cantonese and Wilk could not follow it. He guessed, however, its gist.

Which Shao quickly corroborated. "He is urging them to drive out the foreigners."

"How convenient for us to be driving by," came Wilk's dry comment. It would look as if they were random foreigners who got into trouble, when they had been this man's target all along. There was no mistaking that.

Bowler-man suddenly pulled out a knife and held it up in the air, screaming something. "Death to foreigners, I would guess?" asked Wilk. Shao ignored him, shouting at his driver. Too late to urge him to get out of there. The crowd had turned toward the car. Several men held clubs. Although he could not see them, Wilk assumed there were also knives.

He stood and pulled out his revolver in one smooth movement, taking aim at the speech-maker and firing without hesitation. The man spun and fell back into the fountain. The crowd scattered in all directions.

"Now get us the hell out of here," Wilk said, taking his seat.

"Did you kill him?" whispered Shao, at least half a minute later.

"Looked like he took it in the shoulder. What do you think, Chappy?"

"The left shoulder it was. You aimed for it?"

"I did. It's probably unwise to leave dead bodies behind us." He turned to his companion in the rear seat. "Will you need to make a report of this when we get back to the school?"

"I should. The commandant should know of it."

"I suspect he will use his own discretion about saying anything to the police in Canton."

Shao nodded slowly. "I suppose so. But word will surely go to his military superiors."

"As it should." The man he had shot was almost certainly an agent. It was entirely likely that some in the mob had also been hired thugs. For whom they worked he had no idea, nor was it his concern. Leave that to Major Li's superiors.

The captain sat some time before speaking again. "My full name is Shao Li-jie but we Chinese do not use our given names, for the most part, except with close friends. Shao is good enough most of the time but I do consider you a friend, Jean Wilk."

"And I am honored to call you a friend, Li-jie."

They had moved onto a wider street, leading away from the center of the city. "You acted decisively while I allowed myself to become confused," Shao said after a while.

"It's just experience," Wilk replied and then chuckled. "Well, not *just* experience, but that plays a part."

Shao pondered for a moment. "As when those men shot at our

157

planes, you chose the logical course. And I — I let my emotions take over."

"There is a time for each," said Wilk. He hadn't always gotten it right either, had he? Had his 'logical course' led him here?

He decided a change of subject was called for. "I'll see if there is any hope for the motorbike's engine when I get a chance. If not, perhaps I can find a new one."

"You have worked on cycles before, you said?"

"I built my first myself, fitting an engine to a bicycle." He had been fourteen at the time. Ten years ago. No, make that eleven. "Among other items, my family's firm imported bicycles. They were manufactured for us in Belgium, with our name on them."

"Patrowhatsit?" asked Chappy.

"No, Patrician. That name was used for several lines we distributed, mostly to Polish customers."

"And are you going to go home one of these days, Jean, and sell Patrician bicycles to your neighbors?"

"Perhaps I shall." That would be logical course, after all. Wouldn't it?

36.

Chappy looked up from his newspaper. "The Reds have taken Omsk."

"Then the war is pretty much over." Other than the inevitable mopping-up.

"One war," observed Chappy and returned to his reading.

There was enough war going on right here in the nation of China — if the fractured China could even be named a nation. Two governments vying for dominance and, below them, warlords battling. Perhaps the regime currently ruling from Canton had the most legitimacy; at least it seemed the least of many evils to Wilk.

And he was here. He was willing to serve for a time, to settle into his routine of teaching.

He had taken the opportunity to go aloft at least once in every airplane at the field over the past weeks. This was, in part, to convince himself of their airworthiness and the condition of their engines. Major Li had asked this of him.

Li might not actually know what to do with him. Wilk thought maybe he was being checked out for his own airworthiness. In turn, he flew each Caudron, each Avro, the lone Salmson. The latter proved a more satisfactory machine than he had expected. He still had reservations about its power plant.

There was also a Curtiss biplane from America, sitting forlorn on the edge of the field. Its engine was beyond repair and no new one was available. "The standard trainer in the States," Singleton informed him. "We used a fair number of them in our own schools late in the war."

He wondered what the captain had flown during that war but thought it best not to pry.

Then there was the pair of Ansaldos. Wilk could see why they were fitted as bombers rather than as fighters. They were very fast and strongly built — he admired the engineering of their Warren wing-bracing — but handled poorly. He would not want to dogfight in one.

But each had twin machine guns. They were hardly defenseless.

Some of the other craft carried guns as well. Not the Caudrons, to be sure. The Salmson had both a forward-firing weapon and one for an observer. Some of the Avros also had fittings for a machine gun for the observer and one carried a fixed Lewis gun firing over the upper wing. This was, ostensibly, for the training of fighter pilots.

Wilk would not want to turn any of these boys out in fighters on the basis of what they learned here. He hoped he might be able to remedy that but, so far, he had done little beyond providing them with basic flying skills, and lecturing them on engines and the maintenance of airframes. Their lack of interest in such things was discouraging.

However, in his spare time, he and Sergeant Zhang had undertaken the project of getting the Indian to run. The engine was, indeed, 'bad.' It had proven necessary to mill a few parts for it themselves. Wilk picked up a handful of Cantonese words in the process but it seemed surprisingly unnecessary for the two to actually say anything to each other. Zhang, it must be admitted, picked up a smattering of Polish profanity.

Such was the routine Wilk had fallen into. He lectured two young students, late one morning, on their many failings as pilots when a large black open car rolled onto the field. It carried a driver and four passengers. Two of those were soldiers bearing rifles who immediately hopped down and stood on guard as a man in an officer's uniform descended and looked about.

Some high military official, he guessed. It was not so unusual to have such visitors. Ah, but not with female company. A rather tall young woman in Western dress was stepping out of the rear seat, the officer offering her a hand. She declined to take it.

Wilk peered at them. "That is Colonel Peng, isn't it?" Without waiting for an answer — nor expecting one — he turned to the pair of cadets. "You are dismissed," he announced abruptly, and wheeled to stride across the field toward their visitors.

The soldiers immediately became alert. Only for a few seconds; they knew Wilk from his stop at the colonel's base. Wilk could see Major Li advancing from his headquarters but Peng turned first to him. "Monsieur Wilk! It is good to see you again." The young woman allowed him to take her hand now, as she stepped forward to stand at his side. "Allow me to present my daughter, Mademoiselle Mary Peng. Mary, this is Jean Wilk."

"Oh, the one you wrote me about. I am most pleased to meet you, Monsieur."

"Mademoiselle." Wilk chose to give a slight bow rather than attempt any more intimate greeting. The girl was young. Eighteen her mother had said?

"I still await your visit, Monsieur Wilk," spoke Peng.

"Yes, you must come and help me practice my English." Mary had switched to that language from the French they had been speaking. Now however Major Li was with them and everything proceeded in Mandarin.

"I welcome you, Colonel," said Li. "And Peng's Daughter." His bow was perhaps a little deeper than Wilk's. By now, others had joined them, Chappy included, who gave the colonel a sketchy little salute but did not speak. Peng answered it with a friendly nod.

"I shall intrude only a short while," said the colonel. "I stopped to say hello to my friends, after collecting my daughter from the train station. She is coming home a while from Victoria."

"Father will not permit me to travel alone. He insisted I have a chaperon on the passage from there to the station in Canton. One of the priests we know in Macao. But who," she asked, all mock serious-ness, "will chaperon Father Joao home again?"

"We shall leave that to God," her father told her, "and the Webley Bulldog he conceals in his cassock."

"Surely you will take lunch with me and my officers?" asked Li. "It is nearly time." Lunch was in fact usually a rather casual affair at the air school. Rarely did the officers sit down together and even more rarely with their commandant.

"Gladly. You will include my friend Monsieur Chapman," stated the colonel.

Chappy immediately corrected him. Peng had not been in on the name change. "That's Monsieur Thomas, sir."

Major Li had no objection to that, voiced or otherwise, nor did he seem to care about the name. "Certainly, sir. Might I ask what Peng's Daughter was doing in Victoria?" They all casually strolled toward the major's personal quarters.

"Studying nursing," said that daughter. "Assisting in the hospital, to be more exact. I am preparing myself to study medicine!"

"My daughter sails for France in the spring." The statement was almost a sigh. "She will return to her homeland as a doctor." He glanced down at the hem of her skirt and smiled. "And perhaps with even more startling fashions to shock us."

The hem might have been a good twenty centimeters above the ground.

Mary pursed her lips momentarily in annoyance. "It is the latest style. All the smart girls in Victoria have raised their hems. It is a stroke for female freedom!" She attempted to keep a straight face after that statement but proved unable.

"I saw that 'appenin' back in England," spoke Chappy. "Even before the war ended."

Peng shrugged. "Ah well, we can stand in the way of neither progress nor fashion. But I would recommend you change before your mother sees you."

"Yes, Father." Mary Peng might have a fashion sense but she also had common sense. Wilk found himself liking this young woman with a face that seemed serious one moment and laughed the next. He liked the Pengs. He should visit them soon.

Mrs. Li took the sudden intrusion of so many luncheon guests in stride. Fortunately, she had the services of the base's cooking staff on which to call and as many enlisted men as needed to fetch and carry.

Also fortunately, the students — though officers — were not invited. "You must send me a pilot one of these days, Major," said Peng near the end of the meal. "I have an airplane and none to fly it."

Li's smile was slight. "There are many who ask this of me, Colonel."

Chappy leaned in close to Wilk at that moment. "The colonel asked me on the quiet if I'd like t' go back with 'im," he whispered, "and I said yes. I feel useless 'ere."

"What will you do?"

"Make myself useful."

That was about all anyone could do, wasn't it?

"They could teach me to fly!" Mary suddenly said. There was laughter up and down the table, and she joined in it.

But she was serious, wasn't she? Wilk doubted her father would ever allow it — but in a few months she would be far away and able to get into all the mischief to which young people were apt.

Inevitably, the conversation turned to politics at the end of the meal. Li had produced some sort of cordial. Wilk chose to sip his and let others speak.

"Our republic seems very fragile," someone was saying. "Can it endure the challenges of our times?"

"But China itself is a very old nation," said Li. "It has endured much."

Singleton's cynicism once more showed itself. "Old things have a way of crumbling," he said.

Shao's voice cut through, soft but firm. "A rock may be worm smooth by time yet remain just as hard." Wilk raised his glass to the man, and drank.

Interview, Part Thirteen

"Is that where you got that phrase?" asked Rita Wilkins. "I always thought you made it up yourself!"

"Ah, my secret is revealed."

Our airliner — somewhat smaller than the Seven-Forty-Seven that had carried us across the Atlantic — had risen from Paris and headed east for the last leg of John Wilkins's return to the land of his birth.

"Did your family really sell bicycles?" I asked.

"We did, throughout Polish Germany — Pomerania, if you wish — and in East Prussia, and even across the border in Russian territories. Before the war, that is. Things had to be rethought in its aftermath."

"Especially in light of the Danzig situation, I would think."

"Yes. My father and his partner invested in the new port controlled by Poland. Gdynia, that was. Business then was primarily in the new Poland itself or in the Baltic states."

"A partner? I do not believe I have heard this before."

"His involvement was always kept private. Yet you have heard of his son, my best friend, Theo Trott."

"And his sister," came Rita's voice, softly.

"Yes, Elsa. My fiancee for a time."

Of this I did know. The Trott family had fled Europe, escaping the growing persecution of the Jews. All but Theo.

"Theo died in the war, I understand."

"Executed by the Nazis." His brow tightened only for a moment. "But I came on his murderer in El Plantio and avenged him."

Rita calmly nodded. "And I was there with him."

37.

"We were at the Somme in, mmm — September of Seventeen. Caught the British on the bridges with machine guns and hand-grenades. There was much carnage."

"I remember," said Singleton. "And the next spring our Camels returned the favor there, covering the retreat of the Fifth."

"Yes. I was in that action. Germany's last real offensive."

"Too late."

Wilk nodded. "Too late."

He turned back to their audience. It could have been called an informal class or simply a gathering of their students. The latter, perhaps; flasks of brandy would not have been passed in a class.

"I was high above the fighting," the English flier said. "And wished I could have been higher! My job was artillery spotting in an 'Arry Tate."

The faces of the young Chinese men betrayed their bafflement. Wilk didn't know what he meant either. "Airitate?"

"An R.E. Eight." He pronounced it slowly, distinctly sounding out each syllable.

"Oh. I occasionally saw those, though I was flying close to the ground usually. The English used them in Russia, too."

"What is R.E. Eight, please?" someone asked.

"A fine observation craft from Britain," Singleton told him, with fairly obvious pride. He'd shared a bit of the brandy himself. It was not the first time Wilk had noticed that. "Very stable and easy to fly, but a bit of a sitting duck if the Boche showed up."

"Meaning me," added Wilk.

"But I wouldn't have traded places. I'd rather take my chances with the anti-aircraft guns and the occasional Fokker." Wilk had found the man had a tendency to call all German airplanes 'Fokkers.' "Not down where every infantry rifle and machine gun was pointed at me."

"That was a part of my task." He turned his attention to the cadets. "A task you may be called upon to accomplish one of these days. Unfortunately, with aircraft less suitable than the Halberstadt I flew."

"It's rumored some Brisfits may be headed our way," broke in Singleton. "They'll do the job very well indeed."

"I shot one down once," responded Wilk, to laughter from the gathering. He frowned. "That was not a joke. Killing men is never a joke. But the Bristol fighter is an excellent machine." He would believe they were coming only when he actually saw one.

"In the mean time," said Singleton, "we have the Ansaldos."

Wilk nodded. "Despite the lack of a rear gunner, they could do much damage. Someone to man a flexible machine gun and throw grenades is a definite asset for ground attack."

"But there is something to be said for a quick strafing run," came the other man's response. "As with those Sopwiths I mentioned."

"Or we could just toss hand-grenades from an Avro," came a voice from the back of the room. Captain Shao was leaning in the door frame. "I've found that effective. Are you ready to go, Wilk?"

"I am. Try not to break your necks while I am gone," he told the students.

They were taking one of the Avros. It was equipped with dual controls so, although the distance was not great, they could relieve each other regularly. All the two-seaters at the school had dual controls, of course, for their training role. Some had been built that way, some had the system added — the Salmson, for example. They lifted off shortly after noon and Colonel Peng's airfield appeared below them well before the sun set. They would have all of the morrow there and return to Canton the following day.

It was Mary Peng and Chappy who greeted them, coming down from the veranda. A pair of soldiers joined them at the bottom of the steps, discreetly keeping their distance. "My father is off with his troops somewhere," Mary called to them. "He promises to be back for dinner."

Wilk had descended before Shao and now greeted the approaching pair. "A good afternoon to you, Mademoiselle Peng. And it's good to see you Chappy. Have you been making yourself useful?"

The Englishman grinned. "I've been drivin' Miss Mary around."

"Yes, Chappy has been most useful in my work." Wilk might have inquired as to what that work was but Mary's attention had turned to the Avro.

"Is that the same motor as in Father's airplane?" she asked.

"No, this is a Gnome, but it and le Rhone rotary engine in the Caudron are somewhat interchangeable."

"The Gnome is more powerful, no?"

"It is. There are le Rhones with more horsepower but we have none of those."

Shao stood beside him now. "You should not encourage him, Miss Peng. He would gladly speak of engines the rest of the day."

"And well into night," laughed Wilk. "Better we get ourselves cleaned up before the colonel returns."

Chappy turned his head of a sudden. "I think I 'ear 'im now," he stated.

"Oh, yes," agreed Mary.

Wilk strained to catch the sound of a motor. All he could hear was a sound akin to distant muffled thunder.

"He's in a hurry," observed Shao.

Oh. It was a sound the Pole had heard frequently on his journey across Asia, the sound of hoofs. Before they reached the house, a small cavalry troop rode in, no more than a dozen riders, Colonel Peng at their head. Horses made sense here.

Peng reined in his steed and sat pulling off his gauntlets. How much of his tan uniform was its natural color and how much dust, it would be difficult to say. A saber hung at his side, and his Mauser pistol. A soldier ran to take charge of his mount — a fine-looking sorrel mare — as he slipped from the saddle.

"In time for tea!" he called to them. "Allow me to freshen myself and I shall join you." With that, he practically bounded up the tiled steps and disappeared into his house.

"I would be a lot stiffer than that after riding a horse all day," commented Wilk. "And have been. We should clean up too."

"Same rooms as before," Chappy told them. "I'll go with y'. Miss Mary." He gave the girl a little bow and started away.

"Go ahead," she told the pair of pilots. "I shall also join you at tea."

They in turn bowed, Shao deeply and formally, and followed Chappy. As they caught up with him he said, "The colonel 'as been out chasin' bandits. Some fellow name of Ming 'as been makin' trouble. 'Ere we are."

Half an hour later they sat down to tea on the veranda with Peng and his family. Chappy was with them. Wilk had wondered how intimate he might be with the Pengs. "Will I see you at supper?" he whispered to him.

"Maybe, with you and Shao here. I take tea with them more days than not, but not supper, not usually. That's just the family."

Madame Peng poured the tea. Wilk was surprised to see milk and sugar, in the English fashion. Only Chappy took his that way. Wilk preferred tea with nothing added, unless it be a bit of lemon. "In Russia," he commented, taking the cup Luisa Peng offered him, "they sometimes put butter in their tea."

The colonel, in a fresh uniform, nodded. "I have seen Mongols do this." He paused but a moment before saying, "So, have you a pilot yet for me?"

"You must ask Major Li about that, sir," said Shao.

"I have, more than once." Peng smiled wryly and perhaps exaggeratedly.

Wilk had thought on this from time to time, but not seriously. None the less, he now said, "I could always come up and train one or two of your own men. It would give me a reason to more frequently take advantage of your hospitality."

"You need no excuse for that. But would you be permitted to fly up here?"

"I have another means of transportation now."

"Oh, y' got the motorbike workin'?" asked Chappy.

"With the assistance of Sergeant Zhang."

"Wilk has been roaring about the airfield on it the last few days," said Shao.

"Chappy has been roaring about some himself," Mary Peng said. "He is my driver." She gave the Englishman a rather fond smile. "And my assistant."

"With medical stuff," spoke up Chappy, nibbling at some sort of cake. "Miss Mary goes 'round to the villages and does what she can for folks. I know some about treatin' injuries, 'avin' driven an ambulance, but nothin' about diseases."

"And he provides the protection my father insists I must have," added Mary.

The colonel no more than smiled at that. "I would still prefer one of my soldiers accompany you. Perhaps two of them."

"They make people nervous, Father."

"Bandits should make them more nervous. Though I doubt not that my own men would rob and loot if I did not hold them in rein."

Shao bent the conversation in another direction. "I understand you have been having trouble with bandits, sir."

"There are always lawless men about but this band is something more. Their leader claims to be a revolutionary."

"The Ming Chappy mentioned to us."

"Yes. Ming Zhang-jun, or General Ming as he styles himself though I doubt he ever held an officer's rank in any army but his own." Peng sipped his tea before adding. "He claims to be a descendant of the Ming dynasty."

"Is that possible?" asked Wilk. He knew little of the Ming dynasty beyond the fact that it had existed and ruled. He wasn't even sure exactly when.

The colonel shrugged. "It might be his true name, though I doubt greatly he is the descendant of emperors. Nor would it matter, now the Republic has been established."

"There are those," observed Shao, "who might favor a restoration of imperial rule."

"As it was under the Mings?" Peng shook his head. "It was an age of harsh laws and a rigid society. I would have no desire to go back."

"I sometimes feel we need more order," spoke Shao. The discussion of emperors and republics was left at that.

But Wilk returned to the discussion of Mary's medical endeavors. "Bandits and revolutionaries aside, I would be concerned about the infections to which you might be exposed, Mademoiselle Peng."

"Were there any dangerous outbreaks I would keep her home," stated Colonel Peng. His wife nodded vigorous agreement.

"But that is when I would be most needed, Father! A doctor who avoids sick people is not much use."

"I've heard rumor of cholera out beyond Wuchow," said Shao.

"Under control, according to reports I have received, but its return ever remains a threat. I fear too the return of the influenza." Peng's eyes lingered for some seconds on his daughter. "We lost our son to it. We almost lost Mary."

The long silence following that statement was at last broken by the girl. "That was what decided me to become a doctor."

Shao nodded gravely, perhaps too self-consciously so. "It is not so long since the influenza killed millions, all around the world."

"Nor since the war killed millions more," said Wilk.

38.

"Mary will be staying home through Christmas," said Colonel Peng. "We have taken to celebrating the Twenty-fifth, like the English. There is much of that in Victoria, is there not Captain Shao?"

"There is," he said. "Though Father Christmas has yet to visit our home."

Chappy was not with them for breakfast. Nor was Mary; the word was the pair were preparing for one of their trips to a neighboring village. Wilk, for a moment, regretted that Miss Peng would not be around. Then Axana rose up out of his memories and scolded him for it.

The pangs of loss this had momentarily brought would not keep him from smiling at Shao's quip. "Father Christmas did show up at the Patrokowski home," said Wilk. "Our Christmases could have come straight from a Dickens novel."

"This is your way in Poland?" asked Peng.

"To some degree. Such Christmases are more German than Polish. The Christmas tree is German, you may know."

"Yes, introduced to the English by the royal family." Peng sat a moment, saying nothing, as if making up his mind about something. "Both of you are invited to spend Christmas with us."

"Oh yes," added Louisa Peng, "do stay with us."

"Gladly, Major Li permitting," said Wilk. "I expect to be up here once or twice before then as well."

"Yes, to teach flying," Peng said, rising from his chair. "Shall we meet your students?"

"If they haven't run and hidden," responded Wilk, following in his wake.

Shao bowed to Madame Peng and went with them. As they stepped out onto the veranda he confided to Wilk. "They really only want you, of course. As I was here, Peng needed to be polite to me."

"I doubt they would actually object to you coming," Wilk whispered back. He did suspect the officer was right.

Shao only nodded. A smallish open automobile was parked nearby, next to the telegraph house, being readied by Mary and Chappy, loaded with boxes and bags and rolls of bandages. An Humber, he saw, as he walked over to it. This was one name Wilk was more likely to pronounce correctly than Chappy.

The Colonel only advised his daughter to be careful and moved on. Wilk had his own advice, saying, "Take care of her, Chappy."

They continued toward the ungainly Caudron. The machine did have the doubled controls useful — though certainly not indispensable — for training. Wilk had checked this on his last visit. It had the eight-pointed dark blue star — which to Wilk looked akin to a snow flake — of the Chinese army painted on its twin rudders and wings. This was unlike the airplanes at the school, which carried a star in the five colors of the flag of the republic.

Also unlike the pale bluish-gray machines at Canton, it was unpainted, with a clear dope finish.

"Despite his reservations," Peng announced, "Lieutenant Ye has volunteered to be one of your students. I believe he felt he should be brave enough to do anything an ordinary soldier was willing to attempt."

"I should instruct someone in the care of its engine also," said Wilk. He considered the three men standing by the French airplane, one of them Ye. "Rather than teaching this morning," he continued, "I suggest we carry each of these, um, courageous volunteers up in the Avro and see whether they take to flying. What do you say, Shao?"

"Excellent idea. Why don't I take care of that while you find a mechanic to train?"

The young officer's tone was bantering but Wilk knew he spoke seriously. "So I shall. It would not be a bad idea for all our would-be pilots to learn a little about the engine."

Shao grinned. "And the mechanics learn to fly?"

"It worked for me. Let's meet our students. My students after today,

I guess!" He couldn't expect Shao to come up and help with their training. He wasn't sure Shao would want to come again for any reason.

So the morning went. Peng went about his duties — what were the duties of a minor warlord? — and the pair of aviators introduced their respective students to flight. The Pole attempted to lecture on the le Rhone engine to a couple of Cantonese-speaking mechanics while Shao took the three students aloft. Wilk thought on what his companion had said and decided he would take these two boys up sometime too, if they were willing. That could come with a future visit.

"Only one of them vomited," Shao reported when they broke for lunch. That was nothing unusual, of itself, nor did it disqualify a student. Not unless that student continued to do so on future flights.

"Not Ye."

"No, though he looked a bit green."

They were still eating, lunching on the veranda with the Pengs for it was a fine late-autumn day in the subtropics, when Mary and Chappy returned.

"I got a little blood on my blouse," called out Mary as she breezed past them and into the house. "I must try to clean it at once."

"Allow your *amah* to take care of that, girl," her mother called after her.

Shao's quick frown was as quickly hidden, but not before Colonel Peng observed it. "The captain does not approve of that word, I think."

The young man shrugged, a tad sheepishly, yet his words came out clearly. "It is a vestige of colonialism. It is not even a term from our own country."

"No, it comes from the Portuguese and so, of course, we have long used it."

Shao slowly nodded. "This I understand, sir. But the British use it too and it, well, seems demeaning when they do."

"Perhaps it is," agreed the colonel, "yet there are greater battles to be fought."

"Perhaps it is all the same battle."

"And perhaps you only make it a battle," spoke up Wilk, and chuckled. "I should keep my mouth shut before I make it my battle."

"Sometimes that can not be avoided," said Colonel Peng.

Shao nodded. "We must be prepared to fight when it becomes necessary."

"Indeed. There is a saying that it is better to be a warrior in a garden that a gardener in a war."

"Sun Tzu," spoke Shao. "I have read him."

Wilk sighed. "Yet I would prefer to be the gardener. Or the mechanic. But now I look forward to an afternoon of taxiing the Caudron up and down the field as I introduce my students to its controls."

"I suppose the noise will keep me from napping," complained Captain Shao.

39.

Both men were dead, the student, the instructor. It had happened only that morning, before Shao and Wilk returned.

"And the new students had but arrived and saw it all," reported Lieutenant Cao.

"Had Singleton relatives?" inquired Wilk.

"None that he spoke of. We have a name in England, a brother I think, but we shall simply inform the British authorities in Victoria and leave it all up to them." Cao seemed both satisfied and untroubled, having decided to hand that problem off to someone else. "The major asks that the two of you look over his effects and decide if anything should be sent along. Oh, and a telegram arrived for you, Captain Wilk. I had it left in your quarters."

He had not been able to discourage people here from addressing him as 'Captain.'

"It was rumored Captain Singleton left his homeland in disgrace," murmured Shao as they made their way toward their quarters. "I know not of what sort."

"Nor does it matter now." If it ever had, this far from Britain. Wilk did wonder, however, if the Englishman had been drinking before the accident. Not that flying wasn't dangerous enough as it was.

A yellow envelope rested on the little wooden table by his cot, propped against the rusting wrought-iron electric lamp. The telegram came from Tashkent, from Orkovsky. It was in English: *guide gone stop send letter parents*

Gone? Kasim had said something of leaving, hadn't he? But where? 'Send letter parents' — ah, Kolya must intend to slip more information into a letter to the Patrokowskis. It might be some time before Wilk saw it. That assumed it reached them at all.

Would it be useless to attempt to return to central Asia, to search for Axana? A part of him yearned to do just that. No, that would be foolish. He would return home first. Soon.

WILK

He and Shao made up the entirety of the senior staff now. Major Li might need to take more of a hand in teaching, at least for a while. Oh, the younger instructors did a good-enough job. They were adequate in teaching the basics but none of them had any real experience beyond the school. He'd have to look over the new students.

That came after lunch. Six eager young men. Reasonably eager — that morning's accident might have put a damper on their enthusiasm. Li had already spoken to them; now it was Shao and Wilk's turn.

"What you saw on your arrival happens," Shao told them. "It is a part of flying. We attempt to teach you well so it will not happen to you."

"And it is up to you to learn," added Wilk. "If at any time you wish to quit, there is no shame in it. A wise man knows his own abilities." He looked down the line of faces, faces trying to look confident and unafraid. Wasn't that one familiar?

He glanced down at the list of names and then back at the man. "So you made it here, Lieutenant Ren. Welcome!"

Shao gave him a sidelong look. "You know one of these men?"

"I met Ren at the other end of your country and encouraged him to learn to fly."

"Ah. You came a long way, Lieutenant. Each of you will be assigned an instructor and begin training tomorrow. First, however, you must listen to lectures from Captain Wilk and myself. Perhaps that will teach you something as well."

Perhaps, thought Wilk. But there would always be accidents. There would always be deaths.

There would always be loss.

"So pay attention," he said. "The life you save may be your own — or your instructor's."

Interview, Part Fourteen

"The school was closed down soon after I left China. The newly established Aviation Ministry chose to set up instructional facilities elsewhere. And, too, the Republican government abandoned Canton as its capitol and moved to Shanghai, due to a break with the southern warlords who had supported Sun Yat-sen."

"Did you know Sun?"

"Never met him. Never even glimpsed him. I did have dealings with his successor."

"Chiang Kai-shek."

"Yes. It is most unlikely I would have been invited back in Twenty-seven without Chiang's personal approval. He liked to be involved in every decision — the inability to delegate was one of his shortcomings."

I had to smile. "He had many."

"Don't we all?"

"What was the Generalissimo like?"

"Supreme Commander. Generalissimo is an unflattering translation of his title in Chinese. The man was an odd and complex mix of Confucianism, Christianity, and Corporatism. Too complex, I suspect. Mao presented a much clearer message."

"Then you liked him?"

"Not particularly. I agreed with him on some things and not on others." Wilkins seemed unwilling to add more to that.

"But he, or his government, did ask you to return to China."

"I think my service in the war helped. Chiang admired the German military." There was the slightest of chuckles. "That and the fact that I came from a country with no imperialist ambitions."

"Just as being Polish got you there the first time. What became of Peng then?"

"He was in and out of favor for the next decade or so, and promoted to general. However, his support of Feng's campaign against the Japanese in Thirty-three led to his being forced into exile." He chose to gaze from the window, out over a sea of clouds, for a moment. "It was that campaign that took the life of Mary's first husband."

"Rebecca's birth father."

Wilkins nodded. "A father she never knew."

40.

Another telegram reached Jean Wilk two days later, from Poland. It was brief, as was to be expected: *we worried about you stop good to know you are safe stop come home soon love from all*

Come home soon. He would, it seemed. Where else should he go?

For now, he settled back into the routine of teaching at the air school. The wrecked Avro would not be replaced, or not soon, according to Major Li. Its engine had been removed as a spare, the twisted air-frame discarded. They carried on with the aircraft that remained. Wilk sometimes thought on repairing the Curtiss that had sat unused since his arrival. It would need a completely new engine.

He traveled by motor bike to Colonel Peng's compound, making good time, and better time on his second trip when more familiar with the way. The roads were good, though mostly dirt, running through rolling farmland. It felt good to have the Indian running smoothly beneath him; more satisfying, truly, than flying. He would miss it when he left.

But flying was why he was there — or a good excuse to be there. Indeed, he enjoyed visiting the Pengs. If he left in the gray hour of almost-dawn he could reach them before the heat of the day, give his three students lessons before sitting down to lunch with the family.

Li had not only approved but encouraged these lessons when Wilk presented the idea to him. Perhaps it would not have been so with another than Peng but the men seemed to be friends, or even allies of a sort. Wilk had no intention of puzzling out any politics that might be involved. He would be gone from China soon, after all.

Both the mechanics he was training had been taken up, too, not to teach them flying but to give them an appreciation for it and for the need to properly maintain the engine.

Then it was back to Canton and his duties there. A few days before Christmas Lieutenant Cao came rushing to his plane as he touched down at the end of a lesson. "Major Li wishes to see you at once," the adjutant announced. "It is most important!"

Li was not in his headquarters but stood waiting before their door, holding a piece of paper. "We have received a telegram from Colonel Peng," he announced as soon as Wilk drew near. "His daughter has been kidnapped. He wishes you to come if you can." The hand holding the message fell to his side. "Of course, I agree to this."

Wilk nodded. "I shall go at once, sir." For a moment he considered asking the major if he might take one of the Avros. No, he could reach Peng's compound almost as quickly on his motorcycle, and would prefer having it with him. He went to his quarters immediately to ready himself.

There had been little in Singleton's effects to send along to Victoria, his Distinguished Flying Medal, a wartime photo of him standing beside an airplane with another man. His observer maybe or a fellow pilot. The remainder of his meager belongings were shared out among those stationed at the school.

Wilk himself had chosen a small compass in a brass case. Maybe it would come in handy someday if he knew which way he should go. He slipped it into his pocket now, strapped on his revolver. Nothing more was needed. A few minutes later he was motoring north, along roads with orderly borders of mulberry trees, fields laid out beyond them.

Little of the countryside caught the aviator's eye today; that was fixed on the route ahead as he sped toward the Pengs. Who had taken Mary? And Chappy — was he alright? It was late afternoon, with a velvet purple lying along the eastern horizon, when he arrived.

Wilk was relieved to see Chappy among those who hurried out to greet him. "What happened?" he asked the Englishman.

"Miss Mary was kidnapped while we was on one 'er errands of mercy. It was that Ming fellow."

By then, the colonel himself had reached him, his adjutant in his wake. "We thank you for coming, Jean. I thank you." His formality could not hide the weariness, the touch of despair, in his voice. "We do not yet know what this bandit wants of us."

Chappy spoke up. "The blighter wouldn't tell me what 'e wanted. Turned me loose and said to send someone along and 'e would present 'is demands."

What might this would-be warlord desire? Money? Arms? Medical supplies? All were possibilities. He accompanied the men toward Peng's house. Lanterns were being lit on its broad porch and around the compound. "I would ask you to be one of those who goes to him," said the colonel. "Only if you are willing."

"Certainly, sir. In the morning?"

"Yes, the morning. Chappy was allowed to return with the automobile and can drive you to Ming's encampment. You and Lieutenant Ye." He paused on the steps, turning toward the both of them. "Find out what he wants."

Wilk glanced at the young officer at his side. He could rely on him, he knew. "And return with his demands. Understood."

"Yes. If they are not too unreasonable, agree to them. Ye will know how far I am willing to go." There was a long pause before Peng added, his words measured but vehement. "And when my daughter is safely returned I shall put an end to the man."

"You have fought him before."

"We have only skirmished in the past. He has a large following, outnumbering my own troops."

"But surely not as well trained and armed."

"No, we could have defeated them but it did not seem worth the losses we might suffer. Ming did not seem a threat." There was a bitterness now in his voice. "I see I was wrong."

The sun set behind the willows as they entered the house.

41.

"The colonel hopes a European will impress this bandit. Perhaps he will think the English are involving themselves."

Wilk nodded to this but doubted Ye — or Colonel Peng — was right. The lieutenant was supposed to be the negotiator here, Wilk the adviser. His lack of expertise in the Cantonese dialect, if nothing else, dictated this. But Peng had impressed on the young officer that he should take Wilk's advice.

The country through which they rode, traveling west with Chappy at the wheel of the Humber, was not exactly rugged but definitely more so than around Peng's compound. There were still fields and houses everywhere; this was a populous region. Only the disorganization in China could allow a man such as Ming to operate here.

"This is the village where they grabbed us," announced Chappy, bringing the car to a halt in the dirt lane running among a dozen or so ramshackle houses. Not one villager could be glimpsed. "The directions were to wait 'ere."

But waiting was not necessary. A man on horseback at once appeared from between the houses, trotted over to the Humber, gave a curt order, and wheeled his mount around. Wilk assumed he meant for them to accompany him.

Chappy had picked up Cantonese pretty well, it seemed. He put the automobile into gear and followed the rider. It might have been an hour later when they entered General Ming's camp. Thirty kilometers, perhaps, from Peng's headquarters? Certainly no more, felt Wilk. Within easy striking distance. Easy enough.

And west-northwest from their starting point. He had checked his compass frequently as they rode. Wilk should have no problem finding it by air, if need be. The camp was a haphazard array of patched tents, clustered around a fairly large farmhouse and barns. The roofs of some of these were falling in, the place long deserted by whoever once dwelt here. There were horses penned, as well as farm animals. Future food, undoubtedly.

And, most surprisingly, an airplane. Another of the familiar Caudrons, painted with a crude camouflage scheme, dark green above, sky blue below. Something yellow was painted on the side of the fuselage. A dragon, that's what it was. And at the front of that fuselage, not the typical rotary engine but an uncowled radial. Wilk had seen one like that in Russia, with a ten-cylinder Anzani.

That must be the bandit chief himself emerging from the house. And, by his side, Mary Peng. Ming Zhang-jun himself was a heavy-set man with a neatly trimmed, pointed beard, and pouched eyes. Younger, Wilk decided, than first impressions would suggest. His uniform was simple and unadorned, that of a common soldier. "Welcome to my humble dwelling," he spoke, in heavily accented Mandarin. At least Wilk would be able to understand what was being discussed.

"You are Wilk," Ming stated, glaring at the Pole. "My pilot has told me of you. Fu!" he called out.

The man who came running was one of his own students, one of Peng's soldiers. A deserter now, obviously, and maybe the one who had informed the bandits of Mary's location. He would have only the most rudimentary of skills but he could fly. Wilk had taught him enough. Fu looked decidedly sheepish now when confronted with his former instructor.

"Captain Fu is the head of my air service," Ming proclaimed. The soldier had received a considerable promotion. "But, I would be willing to, ah, name another if you would join my army, Captain Wilk. Make that Major Wilk?" Fu shot him another look, decidedly unfriendly this time.

"That may be discussed at another time, sir," answered Wilk. "We are here on the matter of Peng's Daughter."

"Yes, yes, to be sure. You are Peng's envoy then?"

"I am," stated Ye, stepping forward. "To negotiate, if possible, to carry your terms back, if not."

Well done, thought Wilk. The boy had a head on him. He would defer to him as much as possible. His eyes went to Mary. She seemed well enough. It was likely she was being held in this house before which they stood.

"Yes, the terms." Ming stood as though pondering deep matters, his head down, his hands behind his back, before announcing, "I thought only to demand a ransom, but now I wish Peng's Daughter to become one of my wives. She would know great honor when I am proclaimed emperor."

"Emperor, sir?" Ye could not completely hide his surprise.

"Emperor. I am the heir of the Ming emperors and will restore our dynasty. This is my mandate, to rule China and return it to its greatness!"

Wilk suspected the man actually believed the nonsense he voiced. And there would be those among his officers who would willingly follow along with it for their own cynical reasons.

"Tell Peng this, and that I would have him as an ally as well as a father-in-law. Together we would conquer! And, of course," Ming continued, "I would hope for a dowry. Rifles would be acceptable. Machine guns would be preferable." There was a trace of levity evident in his voice. Whether because he thought he had Peng over the proverbial barrel or was just pleased with himself, Wilk was unsure.

He was sure they were already at an impasse. Never would the colonel agree to such a marriage. Nor would Mary, though it seemed unlikely Ming would ask her opinion. He looked about the camp as best he could without being too obvious. Anything he could learn, anything he could remember, might prove useful.

"This, then, is your demand, General?" asked Ye, managing to remain polite. "You must recognize I haven't the authority to agree to this."

"Then you must carry it back to the colonel," said Ming. "Allow them to depart," he ordered his minions and turned back to the house, Mary Peng and a pair of soldiers following.

"And that is that, eh?" asked Chappy, who had remained in the background. "Back to the colonel?"

Ye only nodded and climbed into the rear seat. Wilk chose to sit in front with his friend, but they spoke little on their return journey.

42.

"We must attack and rescue your daughter," maintained Ye.

Peng agreed. "We will move the men up in the dark. A hard march should easily get them there by dawn."

"How many, sir?"

"All of them." Peng reconsidered that. "Leave the mechanics and such, and impress on them the need to stand guard, if things go wrong. They must be ready to protect the families here." Including Madame Peng, of course, though he said that not.

Ye stood and saluted. "I shall ready them, sir," he said, and departed.

Peng sighed, and slumped ever so slightly in his high backed chair. "I do not expect you to fight, Jean."

"But I will. Allow me to use the airplane. I can attack their camp from the air before you show yourselves, and perhaps distract them."

"Ah, you are an expert on such attacks, are you not?"

"I fear I am."

"I understand. It is a good idea, I think. We will attack at dawn, if possible, whether you arrive then or not." Wilk did not doubt this. "Will you want someone to go aloft with you?"

A gunner? It was hard to use a machine gun from the rear cockpit — from either cockpit — with the Caudron's tangle of wires and tail booms to get in the way. It was even harder to fix any sort of forward-firing gun to it. "I'll take Chappy, if he's willing." The man knew nothing of air combat but he could shoot. Moreover, Wilk trusted him. "Whom I shall ask immediately, with your permission."

"Certainly, certainly. I need to see to my cavalry." The two rose and walked out into in the dimming light of late afternoon, parting company with Peng headed toward the stables, Wilk to the mechanics' shed.

Chappy. Fortunately, the man was with the mechanics as they checked over the Humber. "I might need to follow the soldiers tomorrow," he explained. "Ye wasn't certain about it."

To rush Mary away from the fighting, maybe. Wilk could see that. Maybe it was a mistake to fly. He could get in and out of Ming's camp quickly by motorbike. For a moment, indecision led him to falter.

No, best to stick with his first instinct. To stick with what he knew and leave others to handle the retrieval of Mademoiselle Peng. "I would rather have you in the Caudron with me. I need to fit it with a machine gun and I could use some hand grenades too. Will you give me a hand, Chappy?"

"With pleasure, guv'ner, if it gets Miss Mary back safe. Ye's the man to see about it all."

Ye at once approved their appropriation of one of the Lewis light machine guns and a crate of grenades. He didn't even ask why. With the mechanics' assistance, Wilk soon had a crude machine gun mounting installed at the rear of the Caudron's fuselage, no more than a simple pivoting yoke. That was better than simply leaning the gun on the edge of the cockpit, even if it added a little drag and weight. To be sure, the Caudron had plenty enough drag built into its design.

"You'll have to take care not to shoot our own tail off," Wilk warned Chappy. "There may be no need to shoot anywhere but toward the ground."

There was no more to be done then, so both men grabbed a few hours of sleep. As he attempted to doze off, Wilk told himself he should have borrowed one of the Ansaldos from the school. Those would do a proper job! But he must do with what was available.

Or must he? He rose from his bed and went out into the night. It was overcast and a fairly brisk warm breeze came from the south, suggesting a coming change in weather. Peng's soldiers had marched away a couple hours earlier. The compound felt deserted. Wilk went to the telegraph shed. The operator slept on a cot near his apparatus, always ready for duty, and Wilk shook him awake. The man spoke English; he had already known that. Necessary, maybe, for the work he did.

A few minutes later, a message had been dispatched to the flying school. What would come of it would come of it. Wilk chose not to return to bed, but sat on Peng's porch, dressed and ready to fly. He fell into sleep eventually. The sound of Chappy's boots on the floor awakened him.

"Ready to go," announced the Englishman.

"Me too." They went out to the Caudron, men and machine prepared for flight. Wilk stopped and relieved himself on the ground before boarding. Better than attempting to use some sort of flask while in flight; that was something he had needed to do on a few occasions in the past.

"We should 'ave saved that to drop on Ming's men," said Chappy. "I wouldn't mind pissin' on the lot of 'em! That Fu especially."

A minute later they had the le Rhone engine whirring within its cowling. Wilk headed the airplane into the wind and lumbered into the dark skies. He could feel the extra weight of the Lewis gun as he turned its nose westward.

It shouldn't slow him down, however, not enough to matter. Wilk was fairly certain he would rendezvous with Peng's troops at the right hour. Even at the Caudron's low cruising speed, it should take no more than half an hour, and the faint light of a coming dawn was allowing him to make out landmarks now. He hoped to be able to spy the attacking force before opening fire on Ming's compound.

There was, of course, no sneaking up on that compound. His engine would be heard.

There. A group of horsemen. He turned toward them, flying low. Individual features could not be made out but that was surely Peng at their head, and Peng's sorrel steed. The man on horseback waved and then swung his arm in the direction of the enemy camp. He and his men galloped forward. Wilk rose and opened his throttle, moving out ahead of them. A moment later, Ming's men — those who were awake — saw the Caudron approaching, only seconds after they heard it.

A row of tents. Wilk gestured toward them, hoping Chappy was paying attention to him. A moment later he heard the chatter of the machine gun as he passed over them. Men were starting to organize, here and there, and rifles were being fired. Wilk buzzed one group. A hand grenade burst among them as he rose away and turned back for another pass. Were Peng's men attacking yet?

Yes, there, the cavalry had burst in from one side, and infantry further down, advancing across the open field.

And from that field was rising General Ming's own airplane.

43.

Wilk immediately admonished himself for not thinking to attack the other Caudron first thing and putting it out of service. But was it likely to be of any danger to him with the novice Fu at the controls?

It turned toward him at once. There was a gun, probably another Lewis, but the man operating it was in the front seat. It was possible the machine did not have the dual controls and the pilot had to fly from the rear cockpit. Be that as it may, it did make a difference in the gunner's field of fire. Not a great difference, maybe. And there was no denying the more powerful Anzani made his opponent's plane faster than his.

The two craft slowly circled each other, trying to get into a favorable position for firing. But Fu was not thinking of firing downward. His gunner's position largely prevented him doing so. Wilk could see that at once. The Chinese pilot was attempting to get below him.

So let him. He abruptly — as abruptly as possible in the Caudron — rose to pass above the other aircraft. Chappy released a burst of fire downward. Their opponent veered away, the gunner attempting to shoot in their direction but failing to come close. Chappy leaned forward and yelled in his ear. "We 'it 'im for sure!"

He wagged an acknowledgment and brought his airplane around. "Keep tossing grenades!" he shouted, though he didn't know whether his companion could hear him. Wilk had made certain to have a few hand grenades in his own front cockpit and now searched for suitable targets below. There. He tossed one and returned his attention to the other Caudron without seeing what damage he might have done. Fu's plane might have been hit by the machine gun fire but apparently not incapacitated.

Both machines found themselves side by side, bobbing up and down as their gunners exchanged fire. Then they separated again, both climbing. The Anzani-powered craft had the advantage there — until Fu attempted to climb too quickly and stalled, his lack of experience betraying him. Wilk turned to bring Chappy into a good firing position. A long burst and then another, and the other machine began to spiral down, smoke pouring from its central nacelle. It hit the ground hard.

Time to turn his attention back to the battle on the ground. A sandbagged machine gun emplacement before Ming's headquarters was holding off the attacking force. Had it been there when he visited the camp? Wilk was fairly certain it must have been added in the twenty-some hours since. Maybe Ming expected Peng's answer to his demands.

Wilk motioned toward it and turned to make a run. He found another grenade and tossed it as Chappy strafed the machine gun crew. They didn't get their heavy weapon turned upward in time to fire back. It might not even be set up to pivot that far. An air attack was not something any of these soldiers would expect nor were any likely to have ever experienced one.

The machine gun did spray bullets toward them as they turned away. Their effort had not put it out of commission. Wilk readied himself for another run against it.

What was that approaching? An airplane, surely. Yes, an Ansaldo! His telegram had provided results. Wilk strongly suspected Captain Shao Li-jie was at the controls. It sped past his lumbering craft, diving toward the emplacement with twin guns firing. A bomb was released as the Ansaldo pulled up, landing somewhat behind the machine gun, almost hitting the house.

The idiot! Mary was in there.

But the machine gun had been silenced. Wilk made a sudden decision and glided into a landing close to the house. Foolhardy, yes, but someone needed to get Mary Peng out of there. "Keep 'em busy," he ordered Chappy as he slipped down from the cockpit and sprinted toward the building. He could hear Chappy's gun chatter behind him.

His revolver was in his hand as he entered the house. Fire continued outside; he was uncertain which side had the upper hand. No matter. His goal was to find Mary and get her away from danger. Let Shao

191

provide air support.

No one. Wilk had expected soldiers, guards, at least one or two, but the house was deserted. The sound of a horse whinnying caught his attention. It came from somewhere to the rear. Could some of Peng's riders have reached the house? He found a rear door, opening into a courtyard with stables on two sides, the house on the other. There General Ming struggled with a pair of horses or, more properly, struggled with attempting to force Mary Peng onto one of them while a soldier held their reins.

He was nearly onto them before they saw him, rushing forward, revolver at the ready. The general turned, fumbled with his own pistol, as Wilk stopped, planted his feet and fired. Ming Zhang-jun collapsed, to rise not again, nor have more dreams of mounting the Dragon Throne.

The soldier dropped the reins and fled. Wilk allowed him. "Come," he said. "Let's get you out of here."

Three minutes later Mary had replaced Chappy in the rear cockpit as Wilk piloted the Caudron into the sky. He made Chappy promise to report to her father so he might know she was safe, flying toward her home.

But she waved to him as they passed over so the colonel probably knew anyway.

44.

"I took a few shots at it with my box cannon," Colonel Peng claimed, holding up his Mauser pistol, fitted with its shoulder stock. "Maybe I brought it down rather than Chappy, eh?"

Chappy looked sour but allowed it might be true. Peng laughed. "I will admit is was your kill, Chappy. It deserves a medal!"

Wilk had flown back to the battle as soon as Mary had been safely returned to her mother, only to find the battle over. Shao had landed and stood with them, pondering the wreckage of the downed Caudron.

Wilk's pondering led to a request. "Sir," he asked Colonel Peng, "could I be allowed to take the engine back to Canton?"

"For you I would do anything, Jean. You should know that. The engine will be sent down as soon as I can arrange it." He turned to Shao. "I owe you as well, Captain. It was most fortunate that you showed up."

"Thank Wilk's long and detailed telegram for that," he replied. "I do wish I had arrived in time to see his dogfight."

"I'll be 'appy to never see another," stated Chappy. "Time to 'ead back?"

"It is," agreed Wilk. "And I'll head back to the air school as soon as I reach your compound, Colonel, but I promise to return for Christmas, as agreed." He turned to Shao. "Do you need to refuel?"

The pilot shook his head. "No, I'll fly straight back and see you there. Colonel." He saluted and marched toward his airplane.

"He's going to be a bit full of himself for a while," observed Wilk. "I bid you farewell, sir."

In no more than a few minutes he and Chappy were parting company at Peng's compound and Wilk was speeding south on his cycle, not taking time to make any goodbyes to Mary and her mother. He should be back to Canton before sundown.

Back to his duties, back to everyday routine, for a while longer. Two days later a truck arrived, with a tarp-covered object in its bed. Wilk knew what it was and motioned for Chief Mechanic Zhang to come with him.

He pulled back the covering to reveal the Anzani engine and then pointed toward the flightless Curtiss. Zhang's face lit up and he nodded eagerly.

Grafting the Anzani radial onto the Curtiss could be tricky — it might not work at all — but it was a project to keep him busy until he sailed away from China.

Two or three months? First, Christmas. That was upon them and Li had agreed to him spending several days with the Pengs. He would ride up on a Wednesday, Christmas Eve, and remain through Sunday.

"The Major celebrates Christmas too," Shao confided. "His wife is a Christian of some stripe. Methodist, I think."

"But not Li?"

"I don't believe he can be accused of believing in much of anything, except airplanes and duty. He and I can hold things down while you malinger and eat plum pudding."

"I'll be going for good one of these days." Wilk reminded him.

"So shall we all. Um, perhaps you would remain for Mary Peng, however?"

Mary Peng? What had put that idea into his friend's head? "Mademoiselle Peng is leaving soon too."

"Ah, yes, that is true. Off to Europe, just like you. Well, be that as it may. You leave in the morning?"

"Around noon. I'll teach in the morning."

Shao glanced at his watch. "It's time I taught this afternoon."

Be that as it may, thought Wilk, after the man departed. Did others think he had some interest in Mary Peng? Or even that she was interested in him? It seemed ridiculous. He wouldn't allow such notions to interfere with his holiday.

None the less, he would be careful while visiting the Pengs.

Interview, Part Fifteen

"You married Mary Peng."

"I did, though it first took us fifteen years of hide and seek. She was Rebecca's mother." He gave me a bit of a good-natured squint. "But you know that, of course."

"It would be difficult not to." We both laughed at that. "Rebecca told me all about it when we first met. I think she wanted to make her relationship to you quite clear."

"Ah, of course. When she was in Vietnam in Sixty-six."

"With you. I thought there was a story in you then. Little did I know how many stories."

"And little did I know you were going to steal my daughter and carry her off to America. I've yet to find as competent an employee!"

"Our sons are not so bad," came Rita Wilkins's gentle admonishment.

"But not so interested in carrying on my business. I can't blame them for that. They never knew the world we did, or Rebecca did, for that matter."

"And that might be a good thing."

"Good, bad, who can say? It was just how it was." He turned back to me. "Mary and her father led me to Catholicism, in time." He chuckled. "For better or worse."

An announcement came, in Polish, followed by one in French. John Wilkins, the man once named Jan Patrokowski, peered out the window. "That's Poland beneath us now," he murmured.

The plane began its descent toward Warsaw.

45.

"I shall be returning to Victoria shortly after the start of the new year," said Mary, "and work at the hospital until I must prepare to leave for Europe."

"Perhaps I should fly you down." Wilk meant it jokingly and his tone surely conveyed that fact.

"By all means. My last flight with you did no more than whet my appetite."

Her father's smile was indulgent, her mother's a little less so. "Mary will sail at the end of March," the colonel told him.

Wilk slowly nodded. "That would seem a good time for me to leave as well. You have relatives in Europe?" It seemed unlikely the Pengs would send their daughter to live among complete strangers.

"Several of my family live in Lisbon. And Luisa has a cousin in Paris."

"That is where I am studying," Mary informed him. Not that he did not already know it. "Have we missed any important Christmas traditions, Monsieur Wilk?"

"No, none that are important." Christmas with the Pengs did have all the flavor of one at home, other than the relatively warm weather. And he realized it brought at least a tinge of homesickness. "Aside from there being no church service to attend."

"Oh, Father Michael has promised to visit tomorrow."

"He had to remain in Kanchow for the Christmas Day services," Luisa Peng informed him. "And must return for Sunday."

"A French priest, correct?"

"Yes. He will say mass, of course, but we know you may not wish to attend."

Wilk did no more than nod. He had attended no services of any sort in a long while. He sat contemplating the Christmas tree for some time. It looked a tad barren compared to the ones he had known at home, and had no lights on it. Martha, the housekeeper, entered the room.

She addressed the family in French, saying something about the late hour. The conversation to that point had been mostly in English, for the sake of Chappy even though he rarely joined in. Wilk suspected the man felt out of place.

"Yes, Martha, I shall retire now," said Luisa.

"And I," added Mary.

Everyone rose. "I think I shall step outside for a few minutes," said Wilk. "I thank you all for sharing your celebration with me." He gave the family a slight bow and went out onto the veranda. The sky was clear and star-filled, the wind light but cool, coming from the north. It took him a moment to notice that Chappy had followed him.

Both stood looking out over the darkened field for a time. "I reckon I'll be takin' off soon, too," said Chappy at last. "I won't be needed 'ere anymore with Miss Mary gone."

"Not back to England?"

"I think I'll try out 'Ong Kong. For a while, anyway."

"Maybe Captain Shao can help you out there."

"Maybe." Both stood wordless a while. Then Chappy asked, "Are you plannin' to look for Axana?"

"I am." Wilk felt no need to say more than that.

"Mary asked me if there was someone. She thought maybe there was."

"And you told her?"

Chappy seemed to choose his words with uncustomary care, slowly and carefully answering, "I told 'er there 'ad been. Didn't tell 'er anythin' about it, though, or mention Axana by name."

"Perhaps I should," Wilk said. "I'm going inside now."

The next morning, Friday, Wilk resumed his flying lessons, one student short.

But with two new students to replace Fu, as both of the mechanics he had introduced to flight now wished to learn. He suspected that tales of his air battle might have influenced their decision. Before lunch, a Model T rolled into the compound.

There was no problem recognizing who the driver might be from a distance. The broad-brimmed black hat gave a clue, and his long black cassock was evident when he stepped out of the vehicle. The priest apparently traveled alone. He removed a small satchel from the Ford and walked somewhat slowly toward the house.

Maybe his legs were stiff after the ride. "That will be it for today," Wilk told his students and followed after the new arrival. The Peng women had already come onto the porch to greet him. He was duly introduced.

"Father Michael will say mass for us in the morning and then hurry back," Mary informed him as they followed the priest and Madame Peng into the house. She and Father Michael were deep into a private conversation.

"Your mother is devout," he observed.

"Yet more a practical woman of the world than I am ever likely to be."

Wilk suspected Mary Peng was devout enough in her own way but, as her father, perhaps took her Catholicism with a grain of salt. "Mary is a good Catholic name," he said, intending it as naught but a casual comment.

"I was baptized Mary but my given name in Chinese is Yu-yan. That means 'Beautiful Smile' in English. Mary Peng Yu-yan is how I would state my entire name."

Wilk resolved to continue to address her as Mademoiselle Peng. Or maybe Mademoiselle Mary. It didn't matter. He would be unlikely to ever see the girl again after their roads parted in the spring.

That evening, beside the Christmas tree, surrounded by the Yuletide tokens of another culture, he gave Father Michael and the Pengs the story of his travels, from the leaving of Germany to his arrival here. Of Axana he spoke but made no mention of romance. They might or might not recognize what lay between his words.

He felt sure Mary did.

46.

"Peng is full of his church's social teachings," observed Major Li. "Distributism and that sort of thing."

Wilk knew a little of distributism. He had read both Belloc and Chesterton. "Is anything wrong with that?"

Shao snorted. "It is naive. Nor is it suited to our nation and culture."

"Perhaps not," said Li. "I understand Peng's daughter has returned to Hong Kong."

"And Mr. Thomas with her. I found him a place with my father's newspaper."

Wilk hadn't known this. He was slightly irked Chappy hadn't stopped to see him. "Not reporting, I would assume."

"Surprisingly, a little. He has access to a certain segment of society we Chinese are never likely to completely understand, the lower class Europeans in Hong Kong. But," Shao continued, "his primary duty is delivering bundles of *The Harbor* around the city twice a week."

"That's one way to get to know the place," observed Wilk. He suspected Chappy would turn such knowledge of Hong Kong to some other occupation in time. That assumed the Englishman would remain there. "I shall be running up to the Pengs again in a couple days."

The major knew that of course. Shao might or might not. "Your students are advancing well?" asked Li, more from courtesy than curiosity, he suspected.

"Fairly well. They should know enough by the time I leave."

"Ah, yes. We must have more senior staff, what with your impending departure and Captain Singleton's death. I think some of our junior instructors could be promoted." Li looked to each of them in turn. "I would like both of you to suggest some names. Think about it and give me your suggestions in a few days."

"And perhaps advance some of our students into instructional posts?" asked Shao.

Major Li considered this. "Yes, yes. Give me some names there too, please. A little brandy after lunch, gentlemen?"

Both were entirely willing. "Where did you learn to fly, sir?" asked Wilk, sipping from his snifter.

"At a private school in Japan. They had a single Bleriot monoplane."

"More than a few French pilots had their first taste of flying in one." Wilk had seen some of the craft before the war but not since. A corporal entered quietly, an envelope in his hand, and whispered to the major.

Li nodded and gestured in Wilk's direction. "We have received a letter for you, Captain Wilk. Feel free to read it now." The noncom handed it to him, saluted and retreated from the room.

It was from Poland. Wilk tore it open at once. Not surprisingly, it was written in German, in his father's neat and closely-spaced hand, dated more than a month previously. What a journey these few pages had taken! By rail across Europe, then a ship, French going by the post-marks, through the Suez Canal and on to Hong Kong. It could have been sent as easily the opposite direction.

Dearest Son,

Your mother and I were ever so pleased to hear from you and to know you are safe. All of us were. Everyone is well here but the situation remains somewhat chaotic. Samuel Trott and I are attempting to return to normal business operations but an independent Danzig raises difficulties for us. That is no concern of yours, on the other side of the world!

Young Theo Trott has followed your lead and is studying engineering. Berlin was quite out of the question but there is a good school in Konigs-berg and the family has connections there. He and your cousin Bernard are as close as ever. They both looked up to you, as you are aware. Bernard seemed to be casting about for a direction but now is a pilot in the new Polish air service.

His young cousin had joined the German military as soon as he was old enough and had proven himself as a fighter pilot in the last year of the war. Bernard had almost accompanied Wilk to Russia but chose to turn back at the nebulous border between that nation and Poland. The ongoing fighting with Ukrainian forces there had played a role in the decision.

The Trotts' daughter Elsa is turning into quite the precocious little lady. She is a great reader of anything and everything. Elsa remembers you and hopes you come home soon, as do we all.

Elsa. What would she be, about ten now? Perhaps eleven. He had last seen her, last seen anyone in Poland, in 1917. Wilk had not passed near Danzig when he flew east after the war.

We know you will return. We do not question this. Take care of yourself and may the Lord guide you until you find your way to us and to home.

Now, the letter we received from your friend in Russia: As I do not pretend to understand half of what is in it, I have simply enclosed it. It is short, so it added little weight.

He calls you Jean? We must know more about that when we see you again. Until then, your loving parents.

It was signed by both his father and mother. Wilk set it aside and unfolded the letter from Orkovsky, a single sheet. It was heavier paper than the pages from his father. Those were practically transparent.

The writing was in English.

My greetings to the Patrokowski Family,

I am Nikolai Orkovsky. I was the comrade and friend of your son Jean, in Russia and on his recent journey to China. This letter is, in part, to let you know he is safe and well.

Well when Kolya last saw him. There had been time and opportunity enough to get into trouble since.

I suspect your son will safely return to you soon and wish all the best for all of you. Jean asked (in a telegram) after our guide in the trip across Asia, wishing to know if he and his family were well, I would assume. I must regretfully tell him that Kazimir, as well as his brother-in-law Adrik, have departed from Tashkent. It is said they have relocated in Persia but that seems no more than rumor. I am returning to Russia and am unlikely to hear more of them.

I would most greatly appreciate that you would inform Jean of this. My warmest regards to the Patrokowski family,

WILK

Nikolai Orkovsky

Wilk folded both letters, returned them to the envelope, and finished his brandy.

47.

He was giving the motorbike to Sergeant Zhang. The mechanic would treat it well. The two of them had managed to make the old Curtiss fly too, though Wilk was not willing to advise it be used for training. It looked decidedly odd with the Anzani in place of its original water-cooled vee-eight.

Colonel Peng's big touring car came for him, Mary in the back. To the colonel himself Wilk had already made goodbyes, and to Luisa. Mary would sail from Victoria in two days. Wilk would be on his way as well, maybe not quite so soon but nothing remained to hold him here.

Wilk was to be a guest in the Shao household. Li-Jie had arranged it, was there awaiting him with his parents and the alleged wife. Wilk had never set eyes on the woman. "There will be someone to meet you, Mademoiselle Mary?" he asked, settling onto the leather seat beside her.

"Oh, yes, Father Joao is coming over from Macao. He is an old and dear friend of my father. We shall have rooms adjacent to the cathedral."

"I see. Are you driving us to the railroad station, Sergeant?" he called to the driver. His assumption was they would board a train of the Kowloon-Canton Railway and ride south.

Sergeant Wei was one of the mechanics he had taught to fly. "No, sir. The colonel ordered me to drive you all the way. We shall need to cross to the city on the ferry."

"Yes, the cathedral is in Victoria," added Mary. "But I do think Captain Shao's family lives in Kowloon."

"I know the way, Peng's Daughter. I will take Captain Wilk there on the way back."

Wilk realized he knew nothing of Hong Kong. He should have visited sometime over the winter. At least Chappy would be knowledgeable. So would Mary and probably the sergeant. And Shao, when he connected with him.

The way south was long and wearisome and largely without interest. They bypassed Canton altogether. For some time, he and Mary Peng attempted to engage in conversation but eventually fell silent, watching the paddies pass by, one after the other, each the same.

They crossed a river Wei named the Tung and traveled on, soon finding themselves paralleling the railway, following it on into the British territory. Only Wilk's credentials warranted a second look at the border. Then through increasingly crowded ways, to the ferry, to the island city of Victoria. Wei turned the big car left as they disembarked.

"The hospital where I worked is the other direction," Mary told him. "I shan't see it again for years. I am very frightened and quite exhilarated, both at once, about going to Paris."

"You don't expect to come home for visits?"

She frowned. "I think not. Better not to waste time. When I return to China I shall be Doctor Peng!"

"And I suppose I might be Doctor Patrokowski before long," laughed Wilk. "Doctor of Engineering. That's not as big an accomplishment."

"Big enough, and maybe just as useful. Do you — do you think you will return to China?"

"It's not impossible. I say, is that your cathedral? It's much larger than I expected!" The Immaculate Conception Cathedral was, indeed, impressive.

"It is large, isn't it? You should see the one in Macao! Wait here, Sergeant. Wilk, bring my luggage, will you?" There was a fair amount of it, far more than his own one small bag. It took a little while before he realized she had called him 'Wilk' rather than Mr. Wilk.

But not Jean. Mary Peng was probably not willing to be that familiar. He followed her with his burden, straight through the front doors of the building. It was impressive within, too. Perhaps he had missed something by not visiting cathedrals in Europe. Wilk resolved to do so on his return.

"This is a shortcut," she informed him, going out through a side door near the sanctuary, and on into a sort of courtyard and then into another building. It proved to be an office, with a young fair man in clerical garb at the desk.

"Ah, Miss Peng. Father Joao awaits you." His accent wasn't quite English but Wilk could not place it. "Brother Anthony," he said, holding a hand out to Wilk.

"Jean Wilk." He put down the suitcases and shook. He thought the man's gray habit marked him as a Franciscan.

"Of France?"

"Of Poland." It had been a while since he had needed to explain that.

The man only raised his eyebrows slightly and smiled. "I'm from Ireland myself. We're both far from home."

"I suspect there is a lot of that here."

"Ha, indeed. Well, follow along now." Wilk took up the luggage again, silently upbraiding the friar for not giving him a hand, and trailed behind him and Mary. Fortunately, there was only one flight of stairs. "Here we are," announced Brother Anthony, rapping lightly on a plain wooden door. "This is your room, Miss Peng, but the father said he would wait for you here."

Father Joao answered and at once embraced the girl. He was a small wiry balding man with a closely trimmed dark beard. A fierce nose jutted between fierce eyes. Unlike other Catholic clergy Wilk had seen here — or back in Poland, for that matter — he wore trousers. Black, to be sure, with a black shirt and Roman collar.

"Ah!" he exclaimed somewhat dramatically, turning to Wilk. "This must be the heroic Jean Wilk of whom you have told me." Mary blushed at this.

"Only as heroic as necessary," he replied, once again putting down the bags. For the last time, he hoped.

"And that is the proper way. Anything more is ostentation and pride! Are you remaining with us?"

"No, Father, I have an invitation to visit elsewhere." He turned to Mary Peng. "And I should hurry along and keep neither Shao nor Sergeant Wei waiting."

"Oh, of course. I am sure we shall see each other again before we leave."

"It seems likely," he said, bowed and left. Mary was already engrossed in her conversation with the priest when Brother Anthony shut the door behind them.

"She is a fine lass," stated the friar. "Mary Peng will do good things for her people."

Perhaps she would. Wilk hurried back along the way they had come, but paused a moment in the cathedral's nave, gazing toward the altar, savoring the peace within this place. Then with a sigh, he went out to the patiently waiting Wei.

The sun was setting over the bay waters when the ferry carried them back across to the mainland.

48.

"We have heard your country is at war with the Russians," said the elder Shao. "Since February."

"There was conflict before then, as soon as the armistice was signed." Wilk thought on that a moment and decided it was wrong. "No, well before then, to be honest." Pilsudski's recruiting of Poles to fight Russia during the recent war, what some now dubbed the Great War, had been part of an ongoing, centuries-long conflict.

Shao's family had a decent place a little up the hills above Kowloon. Not so high as the wealthy's homes but not amid the turmoil of city streets.

The offices of *The Harbor*, however, were across the water in Victoria and the senior Shao took the ferry to them each morning. "We name it *The Harbor*," he had told Wilk, "for it is published for all the port cities here, not only Victoria." He was proud of his paper, the paper of which he was an editor and part-owner. That its circulation could be better, he seemed to ignore.

Shao Li-jie had suggested it was out of touch with the nationalism of the times and was probably right. Wilk had no interest in bringing such things up. In fact, were he a resident of Hong Kong he suspected he might read the paper and agree with its editorial slant.

This morning, the three of them were going to the newspaper's offices together. Wilk made a farewell to young Shao's even younger and exceptionally shy wife and followed father and son out. How did Shao travel? A cab?

No. A streetcar. "My father is frugal," Li-Jie whispered to him as they found places in the crowded car.

Maybe I should send him a bicycle, Wilk told himself. He felt it not wise to say it aloud. The streetcar carried them to the harbor and the ferry, and yet another streetcar took them on into Victoria. All about men and and women were bustling. Canton had bustled too but the feel had been different. More tense, perhaps.

WILK

The Harbor was published from the second floor of a nondescript brick office building. "The printing facility is across the street," the elder Shao informed him, nodding somewhere in that direction. Wilk followed both Shaos up a dark stairwell that rose directly from the street level.

And there was Chappy perched on one of the desks and looking well-fed. If the young Englishman weren't careful he'd end up fat. They clenched hands and Wilk pulled him into a half-embrace. "It's good to see you," he said.

"And good to see you, even if you're goin' t' leave again." He reached behind himself to retrieve a slightly crumpled envelope. There's a note from Miss Peng 'ere," he said. "Addressed to you."

Wilk ran a forefinger under the flap, opening it, and looked over the short note. Tomorrow. She was sailing tomorrow morning. Passage had been booked on a British ship, heading through the Suez Canal, via Singapore and Colombo. He handed the message to Chappy.

"You'll come along to see her off," said Wilk, a statement, not a question.

"You couldn't keep me from it. I've grown fond of that girl, I 'ave."

"It is unfortunate," said Shao, "that she must go to Europe to learn medicine. But that will change."

"I think," replied his father, "this is because she is a woman. There are schools in China, perfectly good schools, but not friendly to female students."

"Undoubtedly so, Father. It will be good to have another Chinese doctor, wherever she trains, and be less dependent on foreigners."

Wilk had to smile at that. "So you dislike foreigners?"

Shao chuckled, taking it in the spirit it was spoken. "You are one foreigner I would wish to see remain in our country. We shall hate to see you go, my friend."

"Others, not so much," added Li-jie's father. "Some would prefer China be a colony rather than an equal. Even the British, though they have improved."

"And now the Americans are shouldering their way into a place at the table."

Probably all this was true, thought Wilk, though he did not pay so much attention to such things. Maybe he should. "The late Captain Singleton thought well of the Japanese."

Shao made a face. It might have been comical on another man but he came across as earnest. "The Japanese are as bad as the other imperialists. And we must reclaim Formosa!"

"On that last point, I can agree with my son," said the elder Shao.

"Let me show you around the city today," broke in Chappy. "I'm startin' t' fall in love with the place."

"I'll go with you," Shao Li-jie said. "We shall see you at our home, Father."

The older man's reply was slightly peevish. "I had hoped to pick this adventurer's brain. Later, perhaps, Mr. Wilk?"

"Certainly, sir." Wilk was amused — and slightly perturbed — to be dubbed an 'adventurer.'

"He shall most certainly want to write an article about you," Shao told him when they reached the street. "Several, maybe."

Wilk could no more than shrug. It mattered little what was written about him in Hong Kong. He would not be staying and it was most unlikely to follow him to Poland. They spent the rest of the day touring, first Victoria, then Kowloon, before parting company with Chappy and returning to the Shao home.

The elder Shao did indeed interview him that evening.

Wilk found himself liking the city and, again, regretting he hadn't visited before. He should have made the trip to Macao as well. Who could say, maybe he would return someday.

The next morning he and Chappy showed up early at the cathedral, to accompany Mary to her ship to see her off. A downcast Father Joao went with them. "I have known Mary since she was a little child," stated the Portuguese priest. "Do not think poorly of me if I cry at our parting."

209

"Never, Father," Chappy assured him. "I might just sniffle a bit m'self."

But not Mary and not Wilk. Their farewell was formal, perhaps more formal than either of them actually wished. Then Mary Peng boarded her liner and it made its way from Hong Kong's harbor, bearing her to a land she had never seen.

The three men stood and watched the tugs move it toward the sea. "I pray I live to see her return," murmured the priest. He turned to his companions. "That is in the Lord's hands. I pray also that you remain well, my friends, wherever you choose to journey. Now I must journey back to Macao." He walked away without further words.

Chappy's eyes followed him a moment and then swept the dockside area. "I like it down 'ere close t' the docks. Maybe I could open a shop or somethin' around 'ere."

"Then you intend to stay in Hong Kong."

"When everyone else is leavin'. It'll be you next," said Chappy.

"Yes, I suppose it will."

He should soon find passage on one of these many vessels. Wilk looked out over the harbor. Gulls wheeled overhead.

Interview, Part Sixteen

"It took me months to reach Europe. I took passage on a little steamer with a crew of lascars and made it to the Philippines. There I signed on as engineer with an American ship heading across the Pacific and through the Panama Canal, and another on to Europe."

"And returned home."

"Home? I returned to Poland as I return today, to a very different Poland then and a very different Poland now. Yet I doubt the people have changed much. Maybe they make it my home still."

"Mary Peng went the opposite direction, you said?"

"Yes, her ship passed through the Suez Canal, and undoubtedly arrived in Europe well before I did. I reached Poland in late summer. I was there in time for the end of the war with the Soviets but had no part in it.

"And so it was back to normal life. I did search for word of Axana. For a couple years I searched and heard nothing." His face grew suddenly serious, pensive, as memories returned. "As I searched for Mary after the war with Japan." The Second World War would always be the war with Japan to Wilkins. I had learned that.

I had learned as well not to press him on the subject of the search for his first wife. "You said you did find Axana eventually."

"Quite unexpectedly, a few years later. I don't think we have time for that story now."

Most of the passengers had exited the cabin. "Shall we go?" Rita asked him.

"We might as well," he said, rising from his seat. "Do you think they'll pin a medal on me?"

"You have enough already."

"That's true, my dear." Wilk stopped in the doorway and looked out for a long time before descending.

Afterword

Chronologically, this is the first Wilk novel, set almost thirty years before the events in *The Dictator's Children*. Yet it is also the last one, as we have John Wilkins in his nineties traveling to the newly-free country of his birth.

This is not historical fiction. It is a tale of adventure and romance, and though I have endeavored to be accurate, I am not too worried if I missed something here and there. The tale is set in a chaotic time in a chaotic world. Unlike *The Dictator's Children*, *Wilk* is not a fast-paced, plot-driven story; it is a journey of discovery.

Axana and her father, as many in their region of the world, have both Turkic and Iranian heritage. One is free, of course, to picture them as one will.